"As long as it takes," Stephen had said

Would the marriage last long enough to break her heart again, Manon wondered.

"The wedding is scheduled for Saturday morning," Stephen told her.

"And I've sent a notice to the papers."

"Masterly," said Manon. Things were out of her hands now.

"You said shame killed what we had." Stephen was probing again. "What brought it on?"

She took her time replying and decided against the whole truth. "Circumstances, I suppose," she said finally. "You were away for a couple of days. It all died on me when I thought it out."

"Died on you? I don't think so." He stood over her and lowered his head. His firm cool mouth found her soft one. Manon tried to remain unaffected, but the kiss went on, and she could feel herself responding in the old way....

JENETH MURREY was involved in a near-fatal road accident some years ago that changed her life. During her long convalescence she read romance novels from her local library until she'd read them all. She then sat down and wrote one of her own and went on to make writing her career. She and her husband live in a small North Wales village and enjoy "gypsying" around the continent in their camper during holidays.

Books by Jeneth Murrey

HARLEQUIN PRESENTS
748—DOUBLE DOUBTING
781—HAD WE NEVER LOVED
787—THE DAUGHTER OF NIGHT

HARLEQUIN ROMANCE
2470—THE BRIGHT SIDE OF DARK
2483—HELL IS MY HEAVEN
2559—TAME A PROUD HEART
2567—FORSAKING ALL OTHER
2637—THE ROAD TO FOREVER
2697—THE GABRIELLI MAN
2728—RETURN TO ARKADY
2807—THE WAITING MAN

Don't miss any of our special offers. Write to us at the following address for information on our newest releases.

Harlequin Reader Service
901 Fuhrmann Blvd., P.O. Box 1397, Buffalo, NY 14240
Canadian address: P.O. Box 603,
Fort Erie, Ont. L2A 5X3

JENETH MURREY

bittersweet marriage

Harlequin Books

TORONTO • NEW YORK • LONDON
AMSTERDAM • PARIS • SYDNEY • HAMBURG
STOCKHOLM • ATHENS • TOKYO • MILAN

Harlequin Presents first edition June 1987
ISBN 0-373-10990-3

Original hardcover edition published in 1987
by Mills & Boon Limited

CHAPTER ONE

ON Monday morning, at the exact time specified, Manon Lucas walked across the opulent hotel foyer to the reception desk with an air of smiling self-confidence which was only skin deep. She knew she looked good; she'd laboured over her appearance for nearly an hour just to give the right effect, and she had tried to think herself into a relaxed, optimistic mood so that she could carry her slender height gracefully, but inside she was as nervous as a cat. Her self-confidence had a zero-rating and the smile which looked so natural was nothing but a mask. It curved her full, soft mouth admirably, but it didn't reach her long, wide-spaced eyes which held apprehension and a trace of fear in their hazel depths. Nevertheless, training told, she assured herself. All she had to do was make a blank of her mind, pretend this was an opening night and sweep from the wings to centre stage before she broke into her opening speech.

'Miss Manon Lucas,' she said clearly to the clerk, 'to see Mr Stephan Vestris, by appointment.'

'Yes madam, certainly madam, you're expected.' The clerk grovelled mentally, and she caught the sly, assessing look in his eyes—one of the people who adjusted their servility to the number of noughts they mentally put on one's bank balance—and the idea so tickled her sense of humour that she gave him a dazzling, totally genuine smile and watched him wilt.

5

On the other hand, this syrupy air of reverence probably had nothing to do with her at all; maybe it was just the backwash from the name of the man she had come to see: Stephan Vestris, financier and reputed millionaire with a finger in hundreds of pies. His name meant money, and that impressed people.

It didn't impress Manon, it made her fighting mad, especially since he had started to take an interest in the world of the theatre, and in doing so had ruined the upward spiral of her career as an actress. But this was not the time to display fighting instincts; she had told herself that all the way to the hotel in the taxi. This was the time for propitiation, with a bit of deference added to the smile, and above all, no mention, not even a thought, of the past. Even if he raised that subject himself, she had made up her mind to ignore it, to look blank as though it had never happened. In retrospect, it wasn't a period of her life of which she was very proud!

The clerk raised a commanding finger and beckoned to a burly, grey-suited man, who put down the paper he hadn't been reading and marched across to her side where he took up a protective stance. She summed him up as a tough ex-serviceman, possibly Army, and her lips curved into their second natural smile of the day. Good lord! Stephan had got himself a minder to go with the bullet-proof Rolls she had heard mentioned. Manon, metaphorically, dug her toes in.

'If you'll just give me the room number.' She widened her smile at the clerk and gave him the full benefit of her long-lashed, some said beautiful, eyes; turning her back on the man she thought of as a minder, but it had no effect. The grey-suited man didn't retreat, he stood solidly beside her as if the two of them were connected by an invisible cord, and the clerk shook his head.

'Mr Vestris has his own private suite.' More hushed reverence and mental grovelling so blatant, Manon wanted to throw up. 'This person will escort you, madam.'

Foiled and denied the privacy she needed so badly, she moved off ahead of 'this person' swiftly. She was damned if she was going to follow in his wake, but he was directly behind her as she entered the empty lift, his bulk making an impassable barrier to whoever else might want to use it. The door slid shut, they zoomed upwards and Manon bit her lip in frustration. This was carrying things a bit too far, and she began to wonder if perhaps she would be searched before she arrived in the Vestris presence. Blithely, or at least with the appearance of blitheness, she raised her arms and twirled round.

'See?' She did another pirouette in case he had missed the first. Her black silk suit clung lovingly to her extreme slenderness without a crease or a ruck and the small clutch-bag she waved under his nose didn't have an ominous bulge. But then it wouldn't. The soft, thin wallet inside contained only one five-pound note; there was also a flat compact, a small lipstick, a hankie and the letter bidding her to this appointment. 'No hidden weapons,' she chided gently.

Her fingers closed tightly on the bag and the thick, expensive paper of the letter made an ominous crunching sound which nearly destroyed her façade of bright self-confidence. She didn't know why she had brought it with her, she already knew it off by heart, having read it at least a dozen times since it had plopped through the letterbox on Saturday morning. Perhaps it was because it held out the half-promise of a lifeline and she couldn't bear to be parted from it. It was brief, concise and matter-of-fact, but it was in Stephan's own handwriting and that had to mean something, surely!

In it, he had regretted her unsuitability for the female lead, indeed for any part in the London production of *Second Chance*, but he had an alternative offer which she might care to consider, and if she would call at his hotel, blah. . .blah. . . blah, and he remained hers very sincerely, which was a lie for a start. Once upon a time, and for a very short time, he had been hers, but there had been precious little sincerity about it on his part!

A gruff, stifled grunt brought her out of her thoughts and she watched in amazement as her grey-clad companion's broad face broke into a smile and his almost colourless eyes twinkled. Here was a man she could relate to, forty-ish and almost fatherly. She had met the type before in her younger days when, with her family, she travelled from one Army posting to another. Sergeants and sergeant-majors who had served with her father, and they had all seemed to have that same wide understanding of human frailty allied to a calm capability which made almost anything seem possible.

'Hidden weapons?' He gave her a stiff smile. 'I never thought there was, madam. But the boss's suite's on the top floor and the lift doesn't go that far, not unless you know the trick of it. The name's Battle, like in Hastings,' he added helpfully.

'By name and by nature?' She couldn't help it, it slipped out, and she watched the good-humoured grin which made his chunky face look as innocent as a child's.

'Not me, madam, I go strictly by the book. I'm the peace-loving type—anything for a quiet life.'

The lift whined to a halt and he turned his back on her to operate the 'trick of it' to make it start rising again, while Manon deliberated on future actions, and just what she would say to Stephan Vestris when she caught a sight of him.

Over the last forty-eight hours she had drilled herself into a mood of meek co-operation. That was certainly her intention, but if Stephan Vestris said something to upset her fragile, mental balance, she would very likely lose her temper, and she hoped Battle wouldn't be within earshot. Some of the phrases she had rehearsed for that emergency weren't fit for human consumption.

The lift stopped smoothly and she stepped out into the corridor, attempting to wipe her mind clean of expletives. She was an actress, wasn't she? She had failed the audition for the part she wanted, but Stephan Vestris was offering her another. Knowing Stephan, and she thought she did—you can't live with a man for a month without getting to know his mental processes—it was more than possible there would be strings to it; but if there were, she would have to accept with a smile because she had little or no choice.

The moment was fast approaching when she *had* to be a bit humble, or if not exactly humble, compliant. Necessity demanded it, and that way she might just possibly get a better deal for herself. She had been out of work too long and she was getting desperate. Added to the five pounds in her purse, she had about fifty in the bank—not much to show for nearly three years' work, but she hadn't wasted a penny in all that time.

Their parents had set aside money for Harry's education long before they were killed so suddenly in a multiple motorway crash, but inflation had nearly halved its value and the pitifully small earnings of a young actress had been stretched to capacity to make up the difference. She had tried for walk-on parts with TV, but even though she was a member of Equity she had never managed to be accepted by the FAA—the books were always closed when she had applied to get on to the 'extras' list. This had left her with few options, mostly touring, and up until six months ago she had been working almost regularly.

But theatrical lodgings were no place for a young boy, and the constant moving about when she was with a touring company would have played hell with his education, so the boarding-school was a 'must', and, to keep him there had turned her into a female Scrooge. Her clothes looked good, but they were carefully saved from better times; she didn't look as though she was on the breadline, but lately she had felt that the end of her courage and striving was so close she could almost reach out and touch it.

'This way, madam.' The wide corridor looked endless, but Battle's hand was beneath her elbow now, steering her in the direction of a door. Manon flinched, but not at the coming meeting or at the touch of his hand. It was the way he said 'madam' that bothered her. It was almost as though he knew, but if he did, he would be about the only one. Stephan was like an oyster when it came to his personal affairs, as she had good reason to know.

She entered the room with a studied grace and

deliberately wasted time looking around. The years of bedsits and cheap, provincial lodgings which had terminated in her sharing a small flat in London with another girl had made her unused to luxury and space. Not that she had ever been much used to either, even when her parents were alive; Army pay and Army quarters were neither of them very large.

This lounge was huge, nearly as large as the hotel foyer, and decorated in shades of beige which varied from oatmeal to caramel, and the only wrong note was a large, workmanlike desk which took the edge off the luxury of the deep cream-leather couches and chairs scattered about on the acres of toffee-coloured carpet, and detracted from the exquisite floral arrangements which graced the half-dozen or so occasional tables—and it was all so peaceful and quiet. This high up, little of the London traffic noise percolated, and what did was stopped by the double or triple-glazing.

At last, Manon let her eyes slide to the man sitting behind the desk, and she gave him a smile which was a nice balance between awe and confidence. It didn't work, but then she hadn't really expected it to. Behind her, she heard the door close, and sensed that Battle had departed for some other region, and she and Stephan were quite alone.

'Come and sit down, Manon.' So they were to be on first-name terms, and it made her raise an eyebrow. She wasn't sure whether that boded good or ill! But he ignored her faint air of hauteur to flick through a slim folder on the blotter. 'I'm sorry your audition wasn't a success.'

'How could it be?' She widened her eyes mournfully as she sank gracefully on to the chair set ready, glad of its support. Her knees were like jelly, they wobbled so, she didn't think they would hold her up much longer, and she gave him another gently sad smile as all her resolutions to be a cooing dove vanished in a rush of justifiable anger, which was proving difficult to conceal.

'I went to that audition,' she continued, 'practically certain the lead was mine, and then you were there, sitting in the stalls with the fellow doing the casting, which I found off-putting.' She was mildly accusing. 'And I'd hardly read a sentence before you shook your head. In fact, I wouldn't have called it an audition, it was more of a "dismiss on first sight". What have you done to have so much influence that a shake of your head is all it takes? Have you bought the producer?'

'Leased the theatre,' he corrected smoothly, 'and I'm backing the production. I mean it to be a success and you weren't good enough.'

'Bluntly put,' she smiled sweetly, 'but you don't know anything about the theatre.' She had meant her reproof to be gentle, but it came out with a snap and the rasp of angry disappointment. 'Angels rarely do, so why didn't you leave the casting to the experts? I played that part for several weeks in the trial run in the provinces and my notices were good, yet I wasn't even considered for a bit part this time.'

'Good notices for the provinces,' he nodded seriously. 'But not for the London production. For that, I believe we need somebody with more experience. The—er—experts agreed with me.'

'And a big name plus star-rating?' Manon's bitterness showed through. 'How does anybody expect us younger ones to get any experience when all the plum parts go to established stars? I bet the name you're depending on for your success belongs to somebody who's nearly forty, and she'll be trying to play a girl of twenty-one!'

'Rachel Ashe?' Stephan raised his eyebrows and she wished she'd bitten her tongue off before she had made that last, nasty remark. She knew Rachel slightly, as a humble minnow would know a golden carp, and she liked and admired her.

'If it's Rachel,' she conceded. 'I don't mind so much. She's better than good!'

'Thank you,' he said sarcastically, and angrily she bit back the rude things she wanted to say, and as he flipped over another page in the folder and began to read, she took the opportunity to study him. He hadn't changed much in the three years since she had known him so well. Not quite perfection but as near as damn it. Thick, soft black hair on a well-shaped skull, a hawk-like face with very dark, almond-shaped eyes beneath heavy lids; a mouth which promised heaven and hell, but with him, the two things were the same; a tall, slender but well made body with grace to conceal well muscled strength. Quite the most attractive man she had ever known, and for a moment she regretted what she had thrown away. But regret was a waste of time, it got you nowhere.

'The other job', she reminded him delicately. 'The one you spoke about in your letter.' She tapped the clutch-bag and heard the thick, expensive paper within crackle warningly. 'Do I have some sort of a chance for that?'

'Getting desperate?' Dark, heavily lashed almond-shaped eyes met hers, but there was no emotion in them, no sympathy, no encouragement, and Manon slumped a little on the chair. She wasn't handling this well, she should be more definite, but then, she had never handled anything really well. Always, she seemed to let her heart rule her head.

'So-so,' she shrugged, doubting if she really needed to tell him, but he sat patiently, waiting for her to speak. It was one of the things about him which had always fascinated her, his stillness; he really was the most restful man she had ever met. She had once likened him to a spider, web completed and waiting immobile in a corner for its prey to blunder in.

'But it's more than just "so-so", isn't it, Manon?' he murmured. 'My information says your present position is critical.'

Manon knew a moment of doubt and tried to dismiss it before it could grow into a full-blown suspicion. He couldn't possibly have engineered the recent downward spiral of her stage career, could he? It was too ridiculous even to be thought of! She wasn't that important, in fact, she was of no importance at all, and Stephan Vestris didn't spend time and thought on the unimportant. It was true she had blundered into his web once, but she had won free, and she had never tried to make capital out of their past relationship, never asked a favour.

But these were mad thoughts which showed the state she was in. She drew in a deep breath and banished silly imaginings from her mind to concentrate on the simple fact that Stephan was offering her a job which she badly needed.

'I'm waiting for your answer.' He left his chair to come round the desk, lean back against it and consider her gravely, and while he was doing it, Manon considered him back. He had hardly changed at all, not even that damn stillness!

'You know already,' she muttered as the suspicion raised its ugly head once more. 'I don't suppose I could tell you one thing you don't know.'

'Try me,' he suggested. 'Confession's supposed to be good for the soul,' and she heaved a deeper sigh.

'It's not my soul I'm worrying about!' He might be calling her Manon, but she couldn't bring herself to use his name. 'It's the keeping of it and my body together.' Her soft mouth twisted wryly as she spelled it out. 'No part in the play and no chance of anything else, it's the same lately wherever I've applied.' Again she wondered if it was his doing; was he capable of holding a grudge for three years? Common sense said 'no', but instinct contradicted with a firm 'yes'.

'Not much money left,' she continued flatly. 'I've got fifty pounds. I can pay my share of the rent for this month, but after that . . .' she shook her head. 'And there's Harry. I shan't be able to pay his school fees next term, so he'll have to leave. The flat's too small for Polly—the girl I share with—me and a growing boy, and I can't afford a place of my own. I've been offered some work as a photographic model, but it was one of those shady offers, I don't think it's a reputable studio.'

'It isn't, I've checked. Blue movies on the side.' Stephan raised one dark eyebrow at her angry little growl and a smile curved his mouth. 'Surrender, Manon?'

She took her time thinking about it, although the answer was there already, on the tip of her tongue. She damned the fates which had suddenly stopped giving her any options. Just once more, only once, she would like to have a choice. But not this time! This time, she would have to play it his way right through to the end, and no good would come of moaning about it. Alone, she would have managed somehow. One could exist on Social Security; but she wasn't alone. She had Harry to think about— she had to do her best for him no matter what it cost her. That had been a promise she had made to herself when their parents had died, and she had set to work to keep that promise immediately. She had left her RADA course and taken the first thing which offered; a place in an 'Arts' subsidised company putting on classics at the Chichester Theatre.

And in a small way, she had been very successful, the critics had noticed her and after that, she had had no difficulty in joining a touring company playing the northern circuit. It had seemed as though all her troubles were over, she was becoming known, she had even started saving for a rainy day. Only the rain had come too soon.

Now she was unemployed and broke, and Stephan's offer of work was the first she had had in several months. Because of Harry, she didn't have the right to refuse it, whatever it was. She gave a grim little smile. Everything had its price nowa-days, even Manon Lucas!

'Abject surrender.' She heaved a sigh and then raised an eyebrow. 'I don't suppose it'd do any good to fling myself on your mercy?' And at the silent 'No' his lips shaped, she shrugged. 'I need this job desperately, whatever it is.'

'You know what it is, Manon.' There was a smile on his face, but his dark eyes were hooded. Inconsequentially she thought that a lot of girls would give their back teeth for eyelashes like his and she forced a smile to match his, and tried to be sophisticated.

'How hackneyed,' she murmured. 'Victorian melodrama with the wicked Sir Jasper saying, "Aha, me proud beauty! Be mine or I will foreclose the mortgage!" Then I say, "Unhand me, sir. I love another!"' She crossed her hands on her bosom and made her eyes wide and agonised.

'And do you love another?'

'No.' She was quite honest. 'I've had no time to get involved, too busy. But tell me, if I accept, do I play the same role as I played in Chichester three years ago?' and at his faint gesture of assent, she shrugged. 'How, where, when and for how long, but most important—will the pay be enough for my brother's school fees?'

'Not quite as it was before.' Stephan stayed very still, but his eyes beneath the heavy lids glittered with something like triumph. 'Then, we were lovers, but this time we do it properly, we get married,' and at her incredulous little gasp, he continued without a trace of emotion in his voice, 'so the how will be a state of wedded bliss; the where will be wherever I am, the when is whenever we want it and,' he hesitated, 'and for as long as it takes. Also, I'm prepared to be generous: with money!'

Manon had concentrated on only one word. She had heard the rest, and doubtless, when she was out of shock, she would recall and make sense of it, but for now, that one word had rocked her back on her heels. Whatever other gloomy imaginings had been running around in her mind, this hadn't been one of them. 'D-did you say "m-married"?' She couldn't even control the shake in her voice.

'I did, and I don't say things I don't mean.' Stephan shut the folder with a flick of his hand as though he were closing a door. 'I take it you agree?'

'I've no option,' she shrugged. She was over her shock now and could once more play the blasé woman of the world, but with the sting of reproof beneath the sophistication. 'I can't do anything but agree,' she murmured, and raised her head reluctantly to meet his eyes. 'All the way here,' she continued seriously, 'I was thinking about your letter. I hoped it was a real job you'd be offering. I told myself it had to be, that the past was dead and forgotten, but somehow I knew it wasn't. When you're out of luck, that's it, you're out of luck! But I'll be quite honest with you. If it weren't for Harry, you could go to hell and take your offer with you. Does that make any difference?'

'Not a bit, and the past is neither dead nor forgotten. We have some unfinished business. You knew that, my dear, and you also knew I'd exact payment. It's the businessman in me,' his lips set in a thin, straight line, 'saying that debts must be paid.'

'Nobody walks out on Stephan Vestris and leaves him with egg on his face; is that what you mean?' Manon raised a defiant eyebrow, but her eyes were dead with defeat.

'No egg on my face,' he contradicted her quietly. 'How could there be? I was very discreet, nobody knew unless you . . .'

'I never said a word,' she denied flatly. She had been accused of a lot of things, but he wasn't going to add indiscretion to the list! 'How could I? We'd finished at the Chichester, the rest of the cast had gone back to London. My landlady didn't know I'd joined you on that floating palace you called a "boat", she thought I'd left with the others. If it wasn't public egg on the face, it must have been private. My God, what a mind you have! Harbouring a grudge for three years!' Manon's hazy suspicion hardened into certainty and she felt the deadness leave her to be replaced with a fiery rage. 'My bad patch, the one I'm going through now, that has something to do with you? You engineered it out of sheer spite?'

'Exactly!' He was equally angry, he didn't let it show, but she could feel waves of it battering at her as he stopped leaning against the desk to put a hand beneath her elbow, urging her to her feet. 'As soon as it was feasible, I put the wheels in motion.'

'And what made it suddenly feasible?' she demanded sardonically. 'You missed me so much, perhaps? You bastard!' Her voice was choked with rage. 'How did I ever allow myself to get mixed up with a man like you? But then I was always a poor judge of character. When I think what I've gone through lately, the nights I've lain awake praying for the least little bit part. Anything which would bring me in a living wage ... I could kill you!'

Her little tirade had no effect. Stephan merely pushed her towards the door with ungentle fingers. 'I'll show you where you can wash your hands, then we'll have lunch.'

She went unwillingly as he guided her out of the lounge and into a well appointed bathroom. 'Don't be long or the food will spoil.' He held her by the shoulders and his eyes slid over her extreme slenderness. 'You've become very fragile. I think I could break you with one hand.'

'No, you couldn't!' Manon said it angrily to his retreating back. 'I may wilt a bit at times—now is one of them—but I don't break, ever!'

At the bathroom door, he turned and gave her a morose look. 'No, you don't break, Manon, you don't take that chance. You run away!'

Alone at last, Manon removed her jacket and washed her hands. The mirror over the handbasin flattered her, it made her look quite normal and not as though she had been beaten flat into the ground. She had never had much natural colour in her face, so her present pallor didn't stand out; she refused to let herself weep because tears would make her mascara run and she had no means of repairing the damage, and her shoulder-length, chestnut-coloured hair was shining and reasonably tidy in its smooth chignon.

She slid back into her jacket, a part of her relieved the decision had been made. And it had been made in less than half an hour! She had surrendered, but she had had no alternative. Six months ago, she would have hooted with derision at such an offer, at the idea that she should rearrange her life in just a few minutes, go back three years in time and take up where she had left off.

She would be hurt again, she knew it, she could feel it beginning to happen already, but that was the worst about loving a man like Stephan. It was painful, it turned life upside down. Some girls could take a love affair in their stride, walk into it with a smile and walk out with a shrug, but not her, not Manon Lucas! She had to go the whole hog, be committed, be really in love, so that there was nobody else in the world for her and never would be.

And she still loved Stephan—loved him, hated him, needed him; she would do that until the day she died. When they were apart, she told herself she didn't, that she had grown out of it, but here she was, in the same old trap: seeing him, loving him and wanting him until it was an actual, physical pain. Only this time he wasn't pretending any love for her; he couldn't be, to be making this coldly calculating proposition. So the love would be all on one side—hers—and that would hurt even more.

'As long as it takes', that was what he had said, but how long was 'as long as it takes'? Long enough to break her heart all over again? But she wouldn't break this time either, she vowed. She would just collect a few more bruises on her spirit, her self-respect would take another jolt, but at the end, whenever that would be and however it came, she would walk away, not run! She'd show him!

CHAPTER TWO

STEPHAN'S suite included a long, severe-looking dining-room, and Manon was acidly chatty about the amenities, including the waiters.

'They certainly do you proud. All this,' the airy wave of her hand encompassed lounge, dining-room, bathroom and all the other bits she hadn't seen, 'and room service too!' She gave the huge table and the set of a dozen high-backed chairs a withering look. 'You could use this for board meetings.'

'We do, and why not!' He was flatteningly matter-of-fact. 'I head the consortium which owns this hotel. There has to be somewhere we can meet to discuss business, entertain and house our private visitors. Can you think of anywhere more suitable? Now, come and eat your lunch before you die of starvation. I suppose you skipped breakfast as usual.'

Halfway through her lobster bisque, Manon paused with her spoon suspended. 'Harry?' she queried, ashamed of herself for forgetting the most important male in her life.

'Will remain at his school and spend his holidays with us.' Stephan was economical with words. 'I suppose you'll want him at the wedding?'

Almost, she let rip with a fiery reply—that if Harry was excluded from the ceremony he, Stephan Vestris, could exclude the bride as well, she'd rather make blue movies! But she wasn't sure of herself or

22

her ability to handle a full-scale war. Instead, she became halfway co-operative.

'Yes, please.' She made it submissive. 'But I'd like to tell him about it first, if you don't mind. He's twelve now and very grown up for his age, and I wouldn't like to spring a thing like this on him out of the blue.'

'Phone after lunch. You can tell him I'll be down to collect him on, say, Friday. He can stay here if there isn't room for him in your flat. He'll be a surety for your good behaviour.'

'Still covering your bets?' Manon was suspicious, all brought on by his obvious distrust of her. He made no attempt to hide that distrust and Manon thought the future looked gloomy. She abandoned the bisque, she needed something more substantial to rid herself of this floating feeling. 'I've said I will,' she growled softly—but had she? Things had been happening so fast, she couldn't remember.

But Stephan did and she hadn't! He pointed it out hardily. 'On the contrary, you've not said anything. I've had to draw my own conclusions.'

'Does it make any difference?' she shrugged. 'You've got me over a barrel, I can't see that my saying "Yes" would alter anything.' She helped herself to grilled marinated chicken breasts from the heated trolley at her elbow, eyeing the portion with a jaundiced eye, but consoling herself that she could afford to put on a little weight. It smelled heavenly, but she thought it might turn to dust and ashes in her mouth if she allowed herself to think about the future. Better not to think about it, just make the best of it.

'Maybe I thought you'd take it for granted,' she sighed sadly. 'I didn't think I needed to say "I will" considering the position I'm in.' And for Stephan's benefit, she manufactured a saccharine smile which didn't reach her eyes. 'It's so long ago, you'll have to forgive me for forgetting how you like all the i's dotted and the t's crossed.'

'There are certain conventions which should be observed,' he reminded her as he drew a small box from his waistcoat pocket. 'Another convention. Have I got the size right?'

Manon pressed the catch and blinked at a magnificent square emerald flanked by two diamonds, either of which would have been adequate on its own. Unhesitatingly, she snapped the box shut and pushed it back to him.

'I'd prefer something a little less ostentatious,' she snapped. 'Or is this part of the façade?'

'No façade.' A ripple of expression slid across his face, but she couldn't put a name to it. 'Everything about us,' he continued blandly, 'is going to be ostentatious and genuine, right down to where it hurts. I'm afraid you'll have to live with that.'

'Now he tells me!' She sighed aggravatingly, then shrugged. 'You don't paint a very pretty picture, but I've learned to live with almost anything, if I have to. I only wish I could afford to welsh on the deal.'

'But you can't afford it, Manon, so put on your ring—don't carp about the size of it, I could hardly be expected to give you anything less—and finish your lunch.'

He sounded almost amused and she hated him for it, but what he said was practical. This was just another role and there was a sense of fatality about it as she slid the ring on to her finger—it fitted well and certainly looked impressive—and she forked up another piece of chicken with every evidence of enjoyment.

'Now to clear up a few minor details.' They had finished eating and he watched as she stirred sugar into her coffee. 'You'll need a wedding-dress and a lot of new clothes, all equally ostentatious. We can't hope for Emanuel models at this short notice, but I'll give you the name and address of a friend who runs a good dress shop, she'll fix you up with a dress off the peg and whatever else you might need for a week or so. Do you want to phone Harry now, from here?'

'So you can listen to what I'm saying?' The words sounded spiteful and she regretted them. 'Sorry,' her apology was half-hearted. 'No, I shan't ring Harry. I won't explain a thing like this to him over the phone—but I'll ring the Head's secretary and arrange a visit if that's all right with you. As for the shopping, that can wait a day or so.' She frowned.

'Get your priorities right, the shopping comes first.' Stephen was expressionless but insistent. 'Ring your brother's school and arrange a visit by all means, but I want you properly dressed on Saturday.' He watched the emotions play over her face. They ran the gamut from indignant anger to a flushed embarrassment. He ignored the first and pinpointed the last with accuracy. 'Afraid your fifty pounds won't be enough? But you've more than you think, my dear. I had money transferred to your bank account this morning.'

'You were that sure?' Anger shook her, a futile rage, getting her nowhere. Stephan didn't move a muscle and his face gave nothing away, although the atmosphere between them became charged with electricity and she knew he wasn't pleased. But neither was she! 'Are you equally sure,' she purred, 'that I won't hang on to your money while I tell you to go to hell?'

'Who can ever be sure of any woman?' Stephan ground out, and then relaxed, a visible thing, and Manon could feel the tension draining away so that she could breathe freely once more. 'Be sensible.' He was flat and uncompromising. 'I'm sure you'd rather be seen to pay for your clothes yourself—less humiliating all round. Besides, the sum isn't large enough to take you anywhere out of my reach.'

'My fifty pounds is owed, I can't use it,' she answered him quietly. 'But couldn't it be a simple affair? I've clothes enough for that.' She was feeling ashamed of herself, straining at the gnat when she had already swallowed the camel, but she couldn't be generous. 'I won't wear white!' she added defiantly.

'Slightly off-white, then.' A soft laugh, unusual for him, escaped him. 'Stupid! Who's to know?'

'You know and I know,' she retorted. 'and I've a conscience if you haven't! But, if I have to, I'd rather have a quiet do.'

'Afraid not.' A rueful smile quirked his mouth. 'Like you with Harry, I have to consider Fennie.'

'Fennie?' Manon's voice rose an octave and she gave full value to the two syllables.

'My daughter, Fenella, I call her Fennie.' His whole face had softened as if this were somebody pleasant to think about. 'No, you don't know about her; very few people do. She's part of my private life, eight years old and desperate to be a bridesmaid. The rest of my life's an open book,' Stephan shrugged. 'I'm sure you know . . .'

'That you're divorced.' Manon eyed him glassily.

'Everybody knows that! The news reached me eventually, but fool that I am, I'd never connected the "Steve Vestry" I'd known with Stephan Vestris, not for a long time. The sun must have been in my eyes,' she excused herself sardonically.

'And you've no objection?'

Manon shrugged. 'You're rich,' she said drily, while her heart ached, but she had to keep up some sort of a show. 'You've just bought out my objections,' she added. 'Divorce seems to be the in thing nowadays, everybody's doing it, and I can't afford to be old-fashioned.'

She stared down at her plate, not really seeing it, while the hideous memory of the happening which had tarnished her one and only love affair came back to haunt her. One minute she had been in a dream world of love and passion where everything, even love without marriage, had seemed so right, and the next, she had been made to see it as a shoddy, worthless thing. Her bright, shining dream had been broken and the pieces had fallen about her feet; no longer stardust glitter but dull and obscene.

She sat very still until the memory worked itself through to the end. All her regrets weren't worth a damn. Once a dream had been broken, all the tears in the world wouldn't put it together again. Tears hadn't helped then, and Manon had wept enough of them before she had learned to live with the consequences of her first and only love. Only it hadn't been living, just waiting and existing with only the thought of Harry and his dependence on her to keep her going until her waiting was over.

She drew in a deep, shivering breath and dropped her napkin from fingers to numb to hold it. Her face felt frozen into its usual cool expression and keeping it that way made her muscles ache. Escape was the word, and as quickly as possible.

'Have it your way,' she murmured as her eyes flicked from side to side as if she were looking for a way out. 'I think you've covered everything, so now may I go?'

'Battle will take you and I'll be calling for you tonight at eight.' She thought he looked coldly angry. But he seemed not to have noticed any change in her, and he had had the gall to say she wasn't a good enough actress for the London production! 'I'm taking you out to dinner. Be ready, please, I don't like being kept waiting,' Stephan was well into the tyrant act, but Manon no longer cared as she scooped up her bag and rose.

At the door, she turned back to look at him. 'You're sure you won't reconsider?' she asked gravely, and then, with almost a pleading note in her voice, 'You wouldn't care to make it just a job, a real one? I'll do anything . . .'

'It will be real enough, Manon,' He didn't move to touch her, just handed her over to Battle who was waiting. 'I give you my word on that!'

Polly, her flatmate, still in her practice leotard and leg-warmers, roused from a trancelike lotus position on the living-room hearthrug as Manon came into the flat.

'Did you get it?' Her light voice was full of suppressed excitement. 'You've been gone for hours and I was beginning to worry. What's he like? I've heard he's vaguely Eastern Potentatish, but there aren't any pictures of him, ever. Is he nice? Is it a real job or—or . . .?' she grimaced. 'You know what I mean.'

Manon was disinclined to talk about her interview, but Polly was a friend as well as a flatmate. Without her, Manon doubted if she would have survived these last few months. She owed, and debts had to be paid, but at the same time she knew Stephan would want her to be discreet.

'Not Eastern. There's some Hungarian about two generations back, and if by "Potentatish" you mean bossy, yes! As for the job, it's not exactly in my line, but on the other hand, it's not the or . . . or . . . you're worrying about. I took it.' Manon didn't pause on her way through to the kitchenette where she filled the kettle and set it to boil while she spooned tea into the pot. 'The pay's good, I think, we didn't discuss actual wages and the work's not exactly onerous. All I have to do is marry the man!'

Polly nodded in a mockery of seriousness. 'I knew that was how it would be,' she said airily. 'I see through a glass, darkly! Millionaire falls for struggling actress at first sight! Oh, for Pete's sake, Manon,' her voice rose in a screech, 'tell me the truth before I bust!'

'I've just told you.' The kettle squealed to a boil and Manon made the tea carefully with hands which were beginning to shake. 'I'm marrying Stephan Vestris on Saturday morning, so how are you fixed for tomorrow? I'd like you to come shopping with me, I have to buy a wedding-dress among other things.'

'I don't believe I'm hearing this, my ears have gone all funny!' Polly resumed the lotus position and closed her eyes. 'I shall go back to my meditation and in an hour or so, I shall feel better. Then you can tell me all over again, and maybe I'll believe.'

'You'd better believe it.' Manon stirred her friend's motionless figure with the toe of a high-heeled shoe and proffered a cup of tea. 'It's nearly five o'clock and he's calling for me at eight, taking me out to dinner. D'you think my black silk will be good enough to go with this?' And she waggled her beringed finger beneath her flatmate's nose.

'No!' Polly gawped, gulped and overcame her disbelief to be instantly alert. 'You'd better borrow my green velvet, it's practically new, I've only worn it once, and since this is real and not a dream, I shall help you. I'll press it for you while you give yourself a facial.'

'You look like a chrysanthemum.' Stephan had followed Manon down the stairs from the flat and helped her into the car. He looked at her, at the high-necked, long-sleeved sheath of dark green velvet, at the artless waves and curls of her darkly bright chestnut hair; brushed out of its usual chignon to a loose, feathery shower about her shoulders, and he made it sound like a caressing sort of compliment.

'You're pleased with your purchase? I'm so glad.' Manon was a trifle caustic. 'Cheap at half the price,' she added. Later, perhaps, she might regain her optimism, but at the present she felt as nervous as a cat, yet everything had gone smoothly and almost painlessly so far. It wasn't a nice thought, that she had sold herself, but it was one she would have to live with. 'Is this car really bullet-proof?' she wondered aloud.

'Certainly not,' Stephan snorted disgustedly. 'Is that what they say?'

'Mmm,' she nodded, and embroidered on the

truth a little, adding her own supposition to the prevalent rumour, 'That you have a bullet-proof Rolls and a minder to go with it.'

'Fennie's minder,' he corrected her, 'and he'll be yours as well; I can look after myself. I've only borrowed Battle for a few days while she's staying with friends I can trust.'

'I hope she likes me.' Manon shook off some of her depression and it showed, there was a glint of green in her hazel eyes. 'Just as I hope Harry likes her. It's going to be hell if either or both of them develop a case of the hates, and Harry's not of an age to appreciate eight-year-old girls.'

'They'll be all right if you don't interfere.' He made it flat and uncompromising. 'In any case, why are you worrying now? Fennie will follow my lead. She has a lot of love to spare and nobody much to spend it on. As for Harry's opinion, it didn't weigh with you three years ago, and at that time our relationship was irregular, to say the least.'

'So it was.' She gave him a thin smile as she felt some courage returning, and her bluntness was more for her own sake than for his. She needed to put things in their proper perspective. 'But only a brief affair,' she added. 'Less than a month. I must have been the world's greatest pushover, but what you've suggested for us now sounds more like a life sentence. For as long as it takes, how long is that?'

'I haven't decided yet, there are certain imponderables. At least a year, but it could be more.' Stephan shrugged as if it were of no consequence to him.

'Are you going to allow me to work if I get an offer?' she asked bluntly. 'Because I don't want to be out of circulation too long. I'm an actress,' she reminded him. 'If I'm not seen for a while, I'll be forgotten and have to start at the bottom all over again, and I'm not as young as I used to be.'

That sent him into a swiftly muffled shout of laughter. 'One foot in the grave, Manon? You're barely twenty-three. Does the theatre mean so much?'

'It's my life,' she answered with perfect truth. She could have said, 'It's where I hide from reality'. Once out on the boards, the Manon Lucas part of her died temporarily. It was all there in the script, all the motives, all the reasons, and more often than not a happy ending. For those few hours nightly, she escaped into a dream world, and it helped to keep her sane. It wasn't just the worry about money, these last months of idleness had given her too much time to think. She needed work, hard work to take her mind off things.

'Then play the part I've set out for you and I'll see you don't lose by it. No woman has ever been worse off for knowing me.'

'Which must have cost you a fortune over the years.' His cynicism stirred her to an acid sweetness, but Stephan wasn't interested in her pathetic attempt to hold her end up. 'Your women are just insects to you,' she muttered viciously, 'little crawling things you can tread on regardless.'

As the car swept past the glow of lighted shop windows she saw his eyes narrow while his face grew bland except for a crease in his cheek. He was laughing at her! 'There haven't been all that many,' he murmured deprecatingly.

'You mean you count by the dozen and not by the hundred? A few here, a few there, but they mount up.' She gave him the benefit of her best and brightest smile. 'I thought I'd have faded from your memory after all this time, become just one of the girls.'

'You didn't *think* at all,' Stephan contradicted flatly. 'You *knew* there'd be a reckoning. Nobody walks out on me without giving a reason! Three years ago, I asked and you gave. I wouldn't have forced myself on you if you hadn't wanted me, you only had to say. Unwilling women aren't in my line.'

'Is that what all this is about?' Manon demanded hectically. 'Because I walked out of a relationship?'

'We had something good.' He said it slowly as if he were searching for the right words. 'But it wasn't good enough for you. Either that or you didn't trust me. If you had, you wouldn't have crept away secretly as soon as my back was turned. That's something I can't forgive.'

'You can't forgive? I left you a letter,' she interrupted, and at his snort of derision she protested vigorously. 'I did! I explained my reasons!'

It was hard to keep her mind on what she was saying as her memory insisted on slipping back over three years and she was once again in the cabin of his boat, rocking gently at its moorings in Chichester harbour; listening to the cutting voice of the superbly dressed blonde who was sinking gracefully on to the banquette opposite her.

'So you're Stephan's latest little tramp.' The woman had been quite self-possessed, making a mockery of Manon's attempt at dignity. 'I must say, his taste is improving. I'm his wife!' And there had been more, much more. Even an Army life hadn't prepared Manon for the sewer language which fell from the delicately painted lips. Stephan's wife had

made the foulest-mouthed, old soldier sound like a
Sunday school teacher! She had taken Manon's
wonderful love and reduced it to unprintable terms
and then stood over her while she had packed her
case and scribbled the 'goodbye, it's been nice
knowing you' note.

'Thinking what to say, Manon?' His voice broke
in on her waking nightmare. 'It's too late for
excuses. This is another ball game, accept it and
start looking like a woman in love.'

'You kill me!' She accompanied the words with a
slumbrous look from her hazel eyes until his retort
first widened them in outrage and then narrowed
them in sheer desperation.

'I probably will if you don't do as you're told!'

The night-club was one of the best, and Manon
gazed round at various females from the upper five
hundred and decided she looked as good as any of
them, from a distance. If she had wished, she could
have spoken as they were speaking, in the same
clear, cut-glass way, but she didn't wish. She
wanted to fade into the background, become of no
more importance than the flower arrangement on
the table. She wanted oblivion, but the look on
Stephan's face said she wasn't going to get it.

'Smile,' he commanded, and she managed a
toothpaste grimace just as a camera flash exploded
in the gloom. After her eyes had adjusted, she
did the toothpaste thing again and lowered her
mascara-loaded lashes in what she hoped was a
sexy look.

'Everything laid on. You're courting publicity?'
There was nothing sexy about the glow in her eyes.

'All we can get,' murmured Stephan with a loving
look. 'Wave that ring about a bit. If there's another

photograph, I'd like it to be seen.'

Manon flapped her hand obediently, the emerald and diamonds flashed green and white fire and suddenly it all ceased to be real. She could laugh at herself, at him, at everybody and everything. 'Lord,' she chuckled, 'the damn thing's like a beacon! It must have cost a fortune, I hope you've got it insured!'

'An outward and visible sign . . .' he quoted, but she stopped him before he could finish.

'. . . of something that died a long time ago,' she snapped.

'What killed it?'

Manon kept her eyes on the waiter pouring wine, waiting until he had finished before she answered. The less she said, the fewer explanations she gave, the better for all concerned.

'Shame,' and she looked him straight in the eyes as she said it. 'I decided I wasn't really cut out for a seedy little affair!'

'Then you should be glad we're regularising things,' Stephan snapped back.

'Oh, lord! What a conversation for a dinner table,' she murmured as she widened her eyes in mock admiration. 'Is your new-found conscience supposed to put mine to sleep?'

'Nothing on my conscience.' It seemed that nothing she said would stir him out of his immobility. If this was self-possession, she wished she had a ton of it! 'I didn't walk out on you! If you'd only waited . . .'

'I know,' she interrupted brightly. 'You'd have offered me your heart and a share in your bank balance!'

'With the accent on the bank balance,' he nodded

agreement. 'That's what most people will think now,' he added.

'And you don't mind?'

'What people think doesn't bother me. I do what I have to do.'

'But why pick on me?' she almost moaned.

'Killing two birds with one stone,' shrugged Stephan, and opened the menu. 'I'll explain all that later, this is hardly the place.'

The ritual of dinner dragged on for what seemed like hours, full of false smiles and even falser conversation, and Manon was flagging as she climbed the stairs to her flat. Stephan was right behind her and she was tempted to turn on him with a cutting remark about her only choosing the lesser of two evils, but she was too weary, and when she unlocked the door, he raised his eyebrows in an unspoken question.

'Yes,' she answered as if he had voiced it aloud, 'you may come in for a little while if you want to, Polly leads a dance team, they're doing a late-late show this week. You can share my pot of tea, but you can't stay long, I'm tired!'

A cup of hot sweetened tea put some spurious life into her so that she could listen intelligently as he mapped out the coming week.

'Do as much shopping as you can tomorrow morning and be at the dress shop at noon. I'll pick you up there and we'll have lunch. Afterwards, we'll go back to the hotel and you can phone Harry's school. I'll check with my diary and decide when we can go down to see him, perhaps Wednesday. Luckily, it's not so far from my place near Henley, so we'll call in there on the way back and you can meet Fennie. The wedding's scheduled for Saturday morning at eleven, and I've already sent a notice to the papers for publishing on Friday.'

'Masterly!' said Manon, without acrimony. Things were out of her hands now, she was no more than a mindless pawn on a chessboard, being pushed about, and the dull heaviness was back with her, making her slow of thought.

'You said shame killed what we had.' Stephan was probing again. 'What brought it on?'

She took her time replying and decided against the whole truth. Why make waves? 'Circumstances, I suppose,' she said at last. 'You were away for a couple of days, I had time to think about what I was doing—time when I was free of the romantic thing and I could see straight. There wasn't any future in it, not the thing we had. An unknown actress, who'd been playing minor roles in Shakespeare at the Chichester Festival: everybody said I'd learn a lot that way.' Her lips curled in self-derision. 'If only they knew how much I learned! And an obviously wealthy man with a boat in the harbour and time to kill. You knew all about me, I talked my head off, but I knew nothing about you except your name—and I didn't get that right—not who you were or what you did. It all died on me when I thought it out.'

'Died on you? I don't think so.' He stood over her, and using the handkerchief from his breast pocket, he carefully wiped the red from her lips before he lowered his head, and his firm, cool mouth found her soft, unpainted one. Manon didn't struggle, instead she tried to remain unaffected, and succeeded, nearly; but the kiss went on just that much too long and she could feel herself responding in the old way, her breasts hardening until they thrust painfully against Polly's green velvet which was a bit tight in the bust, while an aching need throbbed through her body, making it pliant and responsive to Stephan's slightest touch.

With a little sigh of hopelessness, she wound her arms about his neck, drawing him closer to her; remembering the silliest things. His boat, the way his face felt like sandpaper in the morning; the wavery dazzle on the deckhead of reflected sunlight on the water and how right and uncomplicated everything had felt until reality stepped in and turned it into a nightmare. The nightmare was coming back again, she could hear it, so that she struggled herself free of him in a welter of shame, and there weren't any warm, comforting arms about her any longer, only the sound of his voice and the touch of his hand on the green velvet that covered her breast.

'Liar! It didn't die.' His hand closed over her taut, throbbing breast and she shuddered at the violence of her feelings. The green velvet was like an armour about her, she could feel him through it, but she wanted his hands on her skin. She licked lips suddenly gone dry as his hands slid to her hips to pull her closer against him so that she felt his hard maleness pressing against her, and her eyelids drooped in remembered ecstasy that set her pulses pounding.

'Just a sample.' She heard him foggily through the blood drumming in her ears. 'So be honest and admit what we had is still very much alive. Noon tomorrow, Manon, and don't keep me waiting!' And she stood very still with her eyes shut until she heard the click as the door closed behind him and she dared to open them again. She made a disgusted face as she caught sight of herself in the mirror.

'Weak-minded fool!' she sobbed angrily at her flushed and rumpled reflection. 'Three years and you're still a damn pushover!'

CHAPTER THREE

THERE were tears in Manon's eyes as she hurried herself under the shower and then into bed. The tears were a curious mixture of self-pity, anger and relief: self-pity because she thought fate had treated her unkindly, anger for her own stupidity, and relief that she didn't have to worry about money any longer. Now, she supposed, would be just the time when some producer would offer her a part. Now, when she could no longer accept!

Meanwhile, it was vital she be in bed and, it was to be hoped, asleep before Polly returned. Polly would want to talk, to know everything, so it would be better if she, Manon, could be deep in slumber— or pretend to be—before her volatile flatmate came home. In her present condition, weary and muddled, it would be easy to lapse into an indiscretion of which Stephan wouldn't approve.

But sleep wasn't easy to find, her body was still on fire with a longing for him until it was an actual physical pain that racked her, and her mind was over-active. She heard Polly's key in the door and swiftly rearranged herself with her face turned to the wall, eyes closed and breathing evenly. Her flatmate stumbled around noisily—deliberately?— but she kept up her pretence and finally, from the far side of the bedroom, she heard the creak as Polly scrambled into the other single bed with a gusty little sigh and settled down at last. Finally came a delicate little snore, and Manon grimaced with envy in the darkness.

Polly could sleep, Stephan was probably asleep as well, but she had to stay awake in the darkness because he had woken something she had thought was dead and there was no rest for her. Would he be kind to her? She couldn't hope for anything like the relationship they had shared in Chichester. That had been love, and she didn't think Stephan loved her now, only wanted her and wanted to make her suffer. But she could hardly expect anything else, hadn't he spelled it out with his arrogant, 'Nobody walks out on me!?' But Harry was secure, and if he wanted the Army as a career, she would be able to afford it, so what she was doing would benefit somebody.

And tomorrow, after she had done her shopping, perhaps she would have an opportunity—maybe she would even have the courage to make one—to ask again, and this time more bluntly, about her own future, how long the charade would really last—'a year, possibly longer' was too vague—and if it would be a charade or a twisted variation of the real thing? But she didn't have to ask that, she already knew. It would last as long as Stephan wished, and he would take whatever he wanted because she had never been able, would never be able to deny him anything.

With so little time to zero-hour on Saturday morning, Manon was off balance, counting in hours but hardly remembering how she had spent them.

Already it was Wednesday, she and Stephan were driving down to Harry's school just outside Wantage, and she kept wondering what had happened to Tuesday, but it took her mind off the coming meeting with her brother and the explanations she would have to make. She went over and over them in her mind, rephrasing the sentences, but without success. Whichever way she put it, it was going to sound dreadful.

She had never lied to Harry, except by omission, and how on earth was she going to make so sudden a decision to marry sound reasonable? Her brother might be only twelve years old, but he was no fool. With a little sigh, she started rehearsing again, her face taut with concentration, while unconsciously her lips shaped the words she intended to say.

'Something bothering you, Manon?' Stephan didn't take his eyes from the road ahead. 'You have an aura of misery.'

'I'm just trying to work out how I'm going to break the news to Harry.' Manon shook her head. 'He's not stupid, in fact he's very intelligent and grown up for his age. He's going to smell a rat. No matter how I put it, it's going to sound unusual, so rushed . . .'

'Then don't put it.' He sounded amused. 'Leave the explanations to me. Your brother and I will have a man-to-man talk and you won't have to explain a thing. All you have to do is look happy.'

'Easier said than done,' she snorted, and lapsed into gloom which didn't lift until she was sitting in the small visitors' room, and Harry, looking unnaturally brushed and clean for a twelve-year-old, was shaking hands, but his attention was split. A part of it was for his sister, a greater part for Stephan, and what was left was given to the Rolls parked on the driveway outside the window.

Harry showed signs of being overjoyed by the news, but his sister suspected that more than half his enthusiasm was brought on by the sight of the car. However, he covered it well, not glancing at it more than half a dozen times, and sounding surprisingly adult.

'I'm very happy for Manon, sir.' This was to Stephan, who preserved a careful calm and accepted Harry's congratulations with a grave expression. 'She's wonderful, but she ought to have somebody to look after her properly, and I'm not old enough yet.'

'Drop the "sir", we'll be brothers-in-law.' Stephan smiled a slow smile of encouragement. 'Now that I've broken the news to you, I'll leave you to have a talk with your sister while I make arrangements with your housemaster for you to have a few days off.'

Manon raised her eyebrows at this, Stephan seemed to have changed his mind about one part of the arrangements at least. 'We'd like you to come back with us today,' he added. 'The wedding's on Saturday, Manon wants you to be there and it's only right you should be; your housemaster will understand that. It wouldn't take you long to put a few things together?'

'I wouldn't miss it for the world, sir—er— Stephan.' Harry's pleasure was also uncomplicated until he recalled the complications, then he sobered.

'But hadn't I better come up on Friday night?' He faced Manon with an agonised grimace at the memory of the summer holiday he had had to spend in the small flat and the teasing he had received from Polly.

Manon, who hadn't said a word so far, gave Stephan an equally agonised look over the top of her brother's head, partly praying he would understand, while all the time knowing he would. 'Friday,' she mouthed silently, 'please!'

'Better come today, you can stay at my place,' Stephan got the message and solved the problem in his own way, firmly and without fuss. 'It'll give you a chance to get to know my daughter, Fennie. You'll be seeing quite a bit of her in the future.' And at Harry's look of stoic endurance. 'She's only eight, but I think you'll like her.'

Harry was relieved and it showed. An eight-year-old girl whom he could treat with lofty superiority was infinitely preferable to having Polly treat him like a child. 'Oh, thank you, sir—er—Stephan. I'd like that, if Manon doesn't mind. May I, Sis?'

She nodded dumbly, there was nothing else she could do. Everything seemed to be slipping out of her control, she was swiftly becoming a mere cog in the machine, a nothing! Then Stephan strolled out to see somebody in authority and an awkward silence developed between brother and sister until Harry broke it.

'Are you sure you're doing the right thing, Sis? Although he's better than Fossy's new brother-in-law. I quite like him.'

'Thanks.' Manon was dry of inspiration, she

couldn't think of a thing to say. 'Er—was Fossy's so bad?'

'Ugh!' Harry's overdone shudder and grimace told their own tale. 'He patted Fossy's head just as though he was a kid and kept on about hygiene. We thought he might be a dentist because he told Fossy sweets were bad for the teeth.' His eyes slid to the window. 'Smashing car,' he observed. 'Fossy's brother-in-law had a Granada. A Rolls beats that, doesn't it?'

'Snob!' Manon's chuckle broke the tension between them and Harry reverted to being a normal boy.

'Did you bring anything to eat, Manon, I'm awfully hungry and if we're leaving soon . . .'

'No, I'm afraid I didn't, but go and get your stuff together.' She looked at him fondly. 'I expect there'll be a meal at Stephan's place, I'm not sure how far it is.'

'What's it like?'

Manon shook her head. 'I don't know that either, Harry. I've never been there. Off you go, we don't want to keep him waiting.'

The Rolls ate up the miles back towards London but slowed down outside Henley where Stephan turned on to a minor road which looped around to return to the river well above the town. Surrounded as it was by a high brick wall, the house was invisible, but once the car had passed through the open gates, it came into view; quite modest compared with some of the mansions they had passed. An oldish place built of red brick which had mellowed over the years to a rosy pink, it stood

against a backdrop of trees and was surrounded by
lawns which sloped down to the river where old
willows dropped their long branches in the slowly
moving water. Manon wondered if this was where
she would be living and if Stephan still had his boat.

Battle, plus a large Alsation, was there to
welcome them, together with a small, dark girl who
flung herself down the three steps which led from
the drive up to the porch and into her father's arms
before she spared a glance for anybody else. Only
then did she look at Manon and Harry. Her almond-
shaped dark eyes, so like her father's, showed a
trace of apprehension, but what she saw seemed to
reassure her and she smiled widely, mostly at Harry.

'I'm learning to ride a horse,' she told him
proudly after she had fidgeted through an introduc-
tion to Manon, although her eyes had widened to fill
with a shining delight at the mention of a
wedding—and Stephan had been diplomatic about
that. Manon, he had said, was going to be his wife,
there was no mention of stepmothers.

'Aren't you a bit small for a horse?' Harry asked
with what Manon thought was insufferable superiority, but on Fennie it didn't register. Instead of
being offended, she giggled.

'Well, it's a pony really,' she admitted. 'It's quite
old, a bit fat and awfully lazy, but I don't think that
matters, do you? Are you coming to the wedding?
I'm going to be a bridesmaid. I've a long dress and I
shall have a posy of rosebuds. Would you like to see
my kittens?' She seized Harry's hand and tugged at
it. 'Come on, there's just time before lunch.'

'I think they'll manage.' Stephan steered Manon

indoors as the two young ones vanished into a garden shed. 'That's if your brother can put up with my daughter's chatter. She started at a day-school in Henley, but it was an unsatisfactory arrangement, so now she has private tuition at home, which means she doesn't have anybody of her own age to talk to.

Manon shrugged and got in a dig of her own. 'Poor, lonely little rich girl! But it's obvious Harry doesn't actively dislike her or he'd have told her so.'

'Then, since he hasn't said anything to the contrary, I presume he also approves of me?'

'Probably.' She refused to be lured into a personal discussion, although it would have given her a great deal of pleasure to have pointed out just how much a Rolls-Royce had influenced Harry's opinion of his soon-to-be brother-in-law. Personalities had very little to do with it, any man with a car better than a Ford Granada would have done!

Time didn't lag for Manon. Thursday and Friday sped away almost unnoticed, filled with dress-fittings, and on Friday evening there was an alcoholic hen-party in the flat, arranged by Polly. Manon gritted her teeth, swallowed one very weak gin and tonic, and when, at last, everybody had gone and Polly was comatose on her bed, she decided to take a leaf from Battle's manual; hadn't he said he always played it strictly by the book? Well, she would do the same, so on Saturday morning, in a cream satin gown dripping with lace and carrying a bouquet of bronzy pink roses which felt as though it weighed a ton, she stood beside

Stephan in the register office with a look of
bemused adoration plastered on her face which was
guaranteed to fool all but the most observant.

There was canned music playing softly in the
background and everything had been laid on as
though this were the wedding of the season and not
a brief, purely practical, civil ceremony. Manon
made the few responses demanded of her and was
shocked out of her dreamlike state by Stephan, who
sounded so sincere that he made his trite responses
sound almost like a dedication. She flicked a
startled glance at his face and caught a glint of
humour in his eyes; she saw it but she didn't believe
it! He *couldn't* be laughing at her! Or could he?
Whatever it was, it took some of the chill out of her
stomach so that when he slid the wide, heavy ring
on to her finger, it felt less like a shackle, and her
hands stopped shaking enough for her to make a
perfectly legible signature.

She had just signed herself over to an unpredictable future, and from here on she would have
nothing more to worry about moneywise, but still
she couldn't feel completely at ease, and she crossed
her fingers superstitiously as they left the office to
the strains of more canned music, 'This Is My
Lovely Day'. She sincerely hoped so, but she
couldn't feel real about it! But for good measure,
she added a shy but brilliant happiness to her
expression of adoration as she emerged into the
outside world at last as Mrs Stephan Vestris.

There was no shortage of wedding guests or
photographers, flash-bulbs blinded her as she
posed, returning Stephan's smile of devotion with a

synthetic one of her own which only turned into the real thing at a glimpse of Fennie, resplendent in white silk caught up with pink silk rosebuds and being very serious about holding the bride's long veil clear of the steps. The child needed both hands for the job so she had passed her posy of rosebuds and fern over to Harry, who was manfully trying to pretend he liked carrying it.

Two glasses of champagne and the wing of a chicken from the substantial buffet at the reception—held in Stephan's own hotel—helped, as did Manon's stage training and a brief contact with Battle's staid normality.

'You just go off and enjoy yourself, madam.' His blunt features were blessedly normal. 'The kids'll be all right and Miss Fennie and me'll see that young Harry gets back to his school on Monday. All the best for the future.'

Polly tended to be a bit weepy, weddings always made her that way she said, although she never cried at funerals. And once again, Manon crossed her fingers while she kept the happy smile going. It was bad luck to speak of weddings and funerals in the same breath! Lord, she took herself to task, what was the matter with her? She was becoming a superstition-freak and things were beginning to feel not quite real.

Stephan's touch on her arm and his quiet murmur in her ear brought her out of her gloom to cut the cake. She smiled at some more strangers just in case they were people she knew. Everybody was unrecognisable and she had met and smiled at so many that her face was beginning to feel like a thin plaster mask which would crack and fall to pieces if she relaxed for even a second.

More champagne corks popped and the hum of conversation seemed to increase with each fizzy little explosion until the noise deafened her. She caught Polly's eye and her ex-flatmate sped to her side at once.

'It's time you changed, my pet!' Polly yelled in her ear. 'That man of yours keeps looking at his watch. I believe he'd like to get out of the bear-garden. Your stuff's in a room on the floor above, I have the key and I'll come with you in case you need any help.'

'What's the matter with you?' demanded Polly as she undid buttons and helped Manon step out of her dress. 'You're looking as though you're going to an execution instead of on honeymoon! It can't be as bad as all that. Heavens!' she added forthrightly as she spread out a going-away silk suit in peacock green or blue and laid the discarded wedding-gown carefully on the bed, 'you've got it made, Manon, and he'll take care of you. I should have such luck! Oh look, they've even provided brandy and fresh coffee for the fainting bride.' She seized the bottle and poured generously into the glasses provided. 'Have a snort,' she advised, 'it'll make you feel better.'

'It'll make me feel sick, but I could do with the coffee.' Manon's stomach started to churn again as she hurried about her changing and stamped her feet into the matching shoes. But the face she turned on Polly was quite calm, if paler than usual. All brides were supposed to be pale and nervous, it was expected of them, she assured herself, as she started to repair her make-up with a steady hand. 'It's the central heating and air-conditioning. I'm not used to it,' she excused herself. 'Once I get outside in the fresh air, I'll feel better.'

She and Stephan slipped away quietly, leaving everybody except Fennie, Harry and Battle getting tipsy. Harry and Fennie had been restricted to ginger beer after an initial sip of champagne and Battle had assured her he never drank on duty, that he would guard the children with his life, and that she was going to be the happiest woman in the world. At which Manon tortured her face into one last brilliant smile and allowed Stephan to whisk her away from the hubbub.

The car was waiting and he seemed to be in a hurry to leave. She knew there were only a couple of small cases in the boot, she had packed her own the previous night, obeying instructions to include only what was necessary for a few days. She knew they wouldn't be away for long, but she wanted to know where they were going. Her nervousness was back in force, the future was a closed book, and although she wanted to read it, she was afraid to open the covers. Besides, she was feeling too tired even to think straight. Instead of being over the moon with relief that Harry's future looked settled, she just wanted to sleep, to slide into a black nothingness and cease to function.

Manon did precisely that. The leather smell of the car's interior soothed her. The seat seemed to shape itself round her, and with a little sigh of

thankfulness she removed her chic little hat with its
sweeping bronze plume, pulled a few pins from her
chignon so that her hair fell loose about her
shoulders, and closed her eyes. The future and the
past both dissolved into a blur and she slept, to
awake a few hours later filled with an ugly certainty.

'You bastard!' She looked around at a familiar
scene, opened her door and received a gust of salt-
laden air in her face. 'Why did it have to be here?'

'It's where it started.' Stephan leaned across her
and closed the door to manoeuvre the car into the
parking-space. 'Where better?'

'You like to hurt?' She choked angrily on tears,
refusing to let them fall. 'I was warned, but I
didn't believe even you could be that spiteful! You
must have your pound of flesh. Bringing me to
Chichester of all places!'

'And who warned you and when?' He slid the
questions in while she was still off balance with the
sights and sounds of the small country town all
about her to bring the past back into sharp,
agonising focus. Even the hotel where he was
parked was familiar, they had come here for dinner
several times while they were living on the boat.

'Your wife, who else?' Manon shrugged, answering drearily and without thinking. Then she realised
what she had said, that it had been said and couldn't
be withdrawn, and she became belligerent. 'And
who better to tell me the kind of man you are?' she
demanded hoarsely. 'No hearsay, you see. All first-
hand information straight from the horse's mouth!'

'My ex-wife!' he corrected blandly. 'You've met
her recently?' Stephan was quite cool about it, but

he had become very still. Manon shrugged, opened the door he had shut and struggled inelegantly out of the car to stand in the cool, fresh breeze from the south. The salty tang of it revived her and she managed to look at him sardonically.

'No, not recently!' She nearly put her tongue out at him childishly. 'Three years ago, while I was on your boat. Woman-to-woman, or should I say bitch-to-bitch!' She had ceased to maintain even the pretence of good behaviour. 'An afternoon call while you were away for those few days. And we didn't have an amicable chat over a civilising pot of tea. That was hardly to be expected, was it? To give the devil his due, your wife was most competent, but she'd done it so often before, hadn't she? Rescued you when you were in over your head and wanting out!'

This time, his stillness frightened her, there was a chill menace about his immobility as if he might erupt at any moment, but instead of a toe-to-toe slogging match in the car-park, he moved only to hold her arm firmly and steer her up the few steps to the hotel entrance.

'You can tell me all about it over our pot of tea.' The menace was still there and Manon shuddered from the cold of it. 'We've plenty of time, I've booked us in here for tonight.'

'I won't talk about it,' she refused flatly. 'I've never talked about it. It's a part of my life I prefer to forget!'

'But now's the time for you to remember!' Thick carpet deadened their footsteps as he led her to the desk and somehow, although she heard him, she knew nobody else would catch his low murmur. 'Smile, Manon. We don't want people to think we're quarrelling so early in our married life.'

'I don't care what people think,' she growled through lips contorted into a mockery of a smile.

The hotel was an old one, it didn't run to suites, and the room they were shown into made Manon feel as if she had stepped back a couple of hundred years in time. The bed was a tester, dominating everything else with its twisted pillars, riotously carved head and foot boards and looped-back curtains, but there was space for the usual furniture plus a decent-sized table and two dining-chairs in front of the window. Stephan had ordered tea and it was brought by a maid following on the heels of the porter with the suitcases.

'Anything else you want, sir, just ring.' The girl was quite young and evidently at the impressionable stage; her eyes were starrily romantic. Stephen flicked a scrap of confetti from the shoulder of Manon's suit and gave her the benefit of his slow smile while Manon, as far from centre-stage as his grip on her arm would permit, applauded the effect of that smile.

'Tea and privacy will be all for now, thank you,' he murmured with a fond look at his new wife, who seethed with a mixture of admiration and irritation at the performance. How dare he! She had never felt so embarrassed in her whole life! Just suppose she behaved that way, he would be embarrassed, and with an inner chuckle of spitefulness, she gave him a melting look.

'Darling!' she murmured throatily in her best

aside. 'Isn't this lovely? I just can't wait for us to be alone!' She kept up the burble of nonsense while the maid set the tray down on the table and arranged things, and only dried up when the door closed behind the girl.

'Tea!' Stephan took advantage of her silence. 'And then we talk, Manon—whether you like it or not!'

She gulped down the implied threat with a mouthful of nearly boiling tea and regarded him bellicosely. 'What's there to talk about?'

'Married couples always talk.' He didn't seem to be taking her or her belligerence seriously. 'It's how they grow together.'

'Ah, togetherness. How did I know that was going to crop up?' she marvelled. 'You'll have to excuse me, but I don't want any. There are certain things I'll have to accept, things I'll have to share, but my thoughts—no! You wouldn't like them if you heard them. Just at present, you're my least-loved person. You've admitted you've blighted my career deliberately; you've used that to force me into marrying you, but you leave my private thoughts alone!' And she set down her teacup with a bang that nearly shattered the saucer.

'But it's not your thoughts I want; it's your memories.'

'Ha!' she exclaimed. 'A life on the ocean wave, subtitled *Love in a Cabin Cruiser*. Damn you, Stephan, what do you want, blood? Why didn't you tell me you were married? At least I'd have been prepared! Oh, I know,' she gave him no chance to interrupt, 'you didn't say you weren't married, but that was a sin of omission. You lied by default. If you'd been honest, I could have looked back on our affair with pride instead of shame. It would have been a good memory, one I wouldn't have been so ashamed of.'

'And that's all?'

'Mmm.' She took a last gulp at her tea, but it had cooled too much and tasted vile. 'You could say my ego took a knock, but I recovered eventually. Now it's your turn.' She gave him a synthetic smile. 'Tell me, how long is "as long as it takes"? Your glib estimate of "a year and a bit, possibly longer", is too vague for me.'

'It will be as long as it takes for you to give me a child to replace the one you so carelessly destroyed,' he answered her quietly. 'You see, my dear, we each of us have something to forgive.'

The words were like stones dropping into a still, dark pool; wrinkling the surface and churning up the mud at the bottom to bring memories floating to the surface of her mind from the dark depths where she had buried her grief and her loss. Through the thunder of blood in her ears, Manon became aware of a distinct drop in temperature. The heat of rage left her and she shivered as she sat silent, frozen with shock.

Was there anything Stephan didn't know? Apparently not! This, her best-kept secret, the thing she never spoke about, hardly dared even think about for the pain it brought with it, was no secret after all. Yet she could have sworn nobody but herself, an anonymous doctor and a sympathetic nurse knew about it.

She hadn't known about the pregnancy herself, not until it was nearly too late to do anything about it, and then she had refused to do anything. All she had felt was joy that she had something of her love left to her, and then, overriding everything else, was the necessity to work, to earn as much as possible to tide her over the time when work would temporarily be impossible.

But the accident had happened, and her miscarriage, all hushed up because why make a fuss when the final curtain had fallen and the show was over? Manon's mind clicked over and things started to fall into place. Stephan had had her investigated, the damned toad! She wished she could faint dramatically but knew she couldn't and wouldn't. Instead, her sense of awareness quickened. It hadn't been her fault that she had lost the baby, but he would probably never believe her. He had been convinced that the tale he had been told was the true one and that conviction had possibly been strengthened by the amount of money he had had to pay to get it!

She stared at him as the implications of what he had said finally sank in. For the last few moments she had only been able to think about the past, shuddering away from the things she had trained herself never to think about, but now, his cool, implacable demand sent her thoughts winging into the future. Dear God, surely nobody, not even Stephan, could be so cruel? To insist that she have another child only to lose that one as well!

It would be more than she could stand. Her little lost baby had become a sweet, lingering memory and she had learned to tolerate that memory, but

what he was contemplating would be too savage to
bear. A living child, her child, but she would never
see it, never hold it or watch it grow up! Angrily,
although her anger was directed mostly at herself,
she fought to stop tears welling into her eyes. Once
she had been weak, but not any more. Once she had
been carried away by her own emotions and maybe
she still couldn't control all of them, but this was no
time to show how badly he had hurt her.

CHAPTER FOUR

'YOU'RE actually a member of the human race!' Manon marvelled aloud, but her eyes were a dead, slaty grey and she couldn't control her shivering. 'And you think you know all about me! My, my! Getting all that misinformation must have cost you a pretty packet; good money thrown down the drain,' she added viciously. 'You only had to ask and I'd have told you the truth for free, that's if I could have brought myself to speak about it or even stayed long enough in the same room with you to answer your questions.'

'You hate me that much?' Stephan shook his head. It was the only movement he made, and although she concealed it well behind a vitriotic façade, she found his stillness more frightening than any threat. 'Don't be a fool, Manon. I can still make you feel ... I've only to touch you.'

'So?' she shrugged. 'Write me off as a woman bent on self-destruction, but what you've just suggested is inhuman. Give you another child and then go away and forget all about it?' Her voice rose hysterically. 'And you had this up your sleeve all the time! I only wish I could have afforded to spit in your eye when you sent for me. All I wanted was a job and an adequate salary, but not this job, it's obscene!' She lowered her voice a whole octave and became bitingly bleak.

'I'm not proud,' she told him with bitter irony.

'I'd have cheerfully licked your boots if you'd treated me fairly. Think how that would have boosted your ego!'

'Not funny,' Stephan obviously wasn't impressed at her sick attempt at humour. 'I did say we both had something to forgive. Put another way, we both have something to be forgiven.'

'You certainly have,' she agreed swiftly. 'Not only some one thing but lots of things, and I'm not in a forgiving mood!' Several long seconds passed silently before Manon was sure her voice was steady enough for speech and then the words tumbled from her lips in a spate. 'You're loathsome,' she accused. 'Spying on me—ugh!' and her shiver of distaste was visible. 'But you've wasted your money, your spies have got it all wrong. You've been misinformed, and I think you should ask for a rebate from whichever firm of enquiry agents you used. I was not careless—I was unfortunate! Being in the wrong place at the wrong time.'

'More unfortunate for my child,' Stephan agreed grimly, and she could have killed him for the pain he was inflicting by making her remember. She raised her chin and glared at him as she tried to decide the nastiest way of telling him the truth, but she was too upset to order her words, they came out in a rush, spilling from her lips in a low, savage growl.

'And nearly fatal for me!' She took a deep breath that thinned her nostrils before forcing her voice to the impersonal, clipped hardness which would cover her grief. 'You want to know what really happened? I'll tell you. There was an accident while the company was on tour. It was the final performance, I was playing Millamant in *The Way of the World*—and a flat, a piece of scenery, fell on me.'

'Very pathetic,' he interrupted coldly, 'but even if that's true, you shouldn't have been working at all, not at that time.'

'Really?' She was now in control of herself and could drawl it sneeringly. 'What was I supposed to do? Stay at home alone, knitting little garments while I waited?' She sniffed aggravatingly. 'Your trouble is that you've so much of everything, you're out of touch with the lower orders. I didn't have a home to stay in and I had a living to earn. I needed the money. I was working and saving while I could, not just for myself but for Harry and the baby. Fortunately, we were doing period pieces and the costumes covered a lot of sins. They certainly hid the results of mine!' She added the last remark with bitter emphasis, but Stephan ignored it.

'There was no need for you to work, I gave you an address and a telephone number.'

'But you've forgotten something.' Cynicism oozed out as her lips formed the words. 'I'd learned that the father of my child was a married man, so I was just another unmarried mother-to-be.'

'Whatever you thought you'd learned, it was my child——'

'But would you have admitted it?' Manon interrupted vehemently as she waved him to silence. She had a lot of things to say, a lot of old grievances to air. 'In any case, I didn't want you as a father for my baby. You'd turned out to be not the sort of man I admired after all; I couldn't trust you any more. You'd cheated me once, how was I to know you wouldn't cheat again. No, Stephan, I'd never have come whining to you and I'm not whining now! Maybe, when the time comes I'll be able to do what you ask—shrug it off and walk away without a backward glance, but I'm not giving any guarantees!'

Apart from the once at the marriage ceremony, it was the first time she had used his name. it slipped out without any conscious volition on her part and just the act of saying it made her feel braver so that she could continue. She would say every single thing in her mind, say it just this once and then be done with it for ever. The past would be dead, along with that pitiful little life which had been snuffed out too soon and she could start afresh with no memories to haunt her or corrode her with their bitterness.

'You certainly don't have anything to forgive me.' Memories heaped on memories and the weight of the sadness of them crushed her into a dull flatness so that she became wearily resigned. 'And as for me forgiving you, I've never given it a thought. I've been too busy forgetting and trying to forgive myself! And now,' she rose swiftly, rather pleased her legs were steady enough to hold her, 'I'm going for a walk, I've a lot to think about, like the future and how to play the part of a brood mare without a script.'

All the fight had gone out of her and she felt dull and drab. 'Alone, please!' She had intended it to be emphatic, but it came out almost as a prayer. 'I shall come back, although if you hadn't played God with my career, taking over my life as though you owned it none of this would have been necessary. Given the smallest break, I'd have managed somehow.'

Stephan roused from his stillness at last to button his jacket and tuck her hand into the crook of his elbow. 'You go nowhere alone from now on,

Manon. Better get used to it. Either Battle or I shall be with you wherever you are. Don't look like that,' as she made a moue of disgust, 'as if you're being threatened with shackles. It's a simple precaution I take with my family. Fennie suffers it bravely, surely you can do the same.'

'Your Fennie's probably known no other life,' and her eyes widened as she realised the implications of what he had said and it roused her from her apathy.

'I won't have Harry put in a strait-jacket,' she snapped. 'He's not in this . . .'

'Only to a lesser degree, and I don't suppose he'll even notice.' Stephan took advantage, to her way of thinking. His lips twitched into his slow, heart-stopping smile, a bit rueful this time. 'He is overseen pretty thoroughly at that school already. He's used to it, he takes it for granted, so I doubt he'll realise he's never alone during holidays. There are, you see, certain disadvantages in having too much money. Lack of privacy's one of them.'

The walk was a fiasco. Stephan drove them the three miles to the Yacht Basin at Birdham where he once more parked the car and they walked along the marina. Even though the season was nearly over, Chichester harbour, with more than twenty-five square miles of sheltered water, still had a lot of craft moored both at the marina and off-shore, and a fleet of small sailing yachts, all rigged identically with the same coloured sails, were having a whale of a time tacking back and forth in the evening breeze.

Unconsciously, Manon found herself looking for one particular silhouette. Nearly thirty feet of grace and power; a raking prow; a wide, winged bridge; the gleam of white paint and the shine of varnished wood with the brass letters spelling out *Speedwell* set on a navy blue and gold plaque on the counter.

'Not here any longer.' Stephan caught her searching gaze. 'This end has become too busy and one's always in the way of some club regatta. She's over at Bosham Creek. You remember Bosham?'

'How could I ever forget?' She was bitterly sardonic. 'We met there!' The memory should have been hazy, she had drilled herself never to think about it, but it sprang to life in her mind as though it had only happened yesterday. A Sunday afternoon, no performance that evening, so she had it to herself, and she had taken the bus to Bosham; her guidebook had said it was a must.

A sleepy little village with soft-coloured cottages, standing on a small peninsula between two tidal creeks, it was there that Canute was supposed to have ordered the waves and Harold was said to have heard Mass before he sailed to Normandy to become Duke William's prisoner. Somebody had told her about a yew-tree, propped up and carefully preserved but still alive and green, which had been young and lusty when Matilda had landed to join her Norman Duke. Nobody seemed to know exactly where the tree was, but everybody she had asked thought it might be at Bosham.

Manon had never found the tree. Her little tour of inspection had come to an abrupt halt before she had had a chance to look. Instead, she had met Stephan, he had smiled at her and everything else had ceased to matter. In worn jeans, a white shirt and a navy blue guernsey, he hadn't looked wealthy, he hadn't acted wealthy and, she remembered savagely, he hadn't said he was married!

Stephan was speaking, she had missed most of

what he was saying, only catching the end. '. . . we'll go over and pick her up in the morning, she's all ready to leave.' He sounded satisfied. 'Are you?'

'In clothes like this?' Her hand swept over the peacock suit. 'No, I'm not! You should have told me, I'd have brought some jeans and tee-shirts, not to mention a . . .'

'All aboard, waiting.' He was as economical as ever with words, even slyly humorous. 'A size larger than the last time, you look a bit broader in the beam!'

'I'm not,' she denied furiously, momentarily diverted from miserable thoughts, 'and I'm not going!' From somewhere, she found the courage to be difficult. 'The thought of it makes me sick!'

'Unpleasant associations? I can understand that. My ex-wife would have given you a bad time,' Stephan nodded. 'But the boat holds other memories, better ones.'

'None I want to remember.' Manon fought the tears that threatened to fill her eyes. She won, her eyes remained dry but her voice quivered huskily with the effort. 'Damn you, Stephan, don't you realise it still hurts—or is that what this is all about, hurting me!'

'Give it time,' he advised. 'We've plenty to spare. We could go over there now and still be back in the hotel for dinner. You'd have a chance to get used to it again and I think you'll find it isn't as bad as you imagine.'

But Manon dug her heels in, metaphorically; turning her back on him and walking, almost marching away towards the car-park. In two long strides, he caught her up, fastening his hand on her wrist in a far from loverlike gesture.

'If you won't this evening, you won't. But tomorrow morning, you will.' He made it sound more like a threat than a promise. 'We'll leave early and work our way westwards along the coast. We'll lie up overnight before heading south. The long-range weather forecast is good for this time of the year, we'll try Dinard or St Malo for a few days while we get used to living with each other again.'

After dinner, Manon glued herself to the television in the hotel lounge, pretending an interest in a disaster movie she had seen several times before. Stephan occupied himself with a private telephone in the foyer. He was absent for nearly an hour and she found herself missing him while she sipped lethargically at a gin and tonic.

The alcohol did nothing for her, even though it came on top of the wine she had drunk with dinner. She couldn't blot out the future, and she trembled with suppressed nervousness about what was to come when the telephone was finally hung up and the TV programmes came to an end. Then would be the time of truth, and she didn't want the truth, it would make her see herself and the whole situation as it really was and not as she liked to think it was.

She loved a despicable man; a selfish, soulless; inconsiderate swine without a trace of humanity in his make-up, and when it came to the crunch, she didn't think she could hide it. Better to pretend she was a sex-mad fiend, in the sense that she was addicted to making love with him, than for him to know he could walk all over her if he wished.

A touch of his hand on her shoulder made her jump as though she had been scalded, and when he gently removed the half-consumed gin and tonic from her hand, her cold fingers released it reluctantly.

'Too much of that's bad for the complexion,' he murmured softly so that the two other aged residents, hypnotised by the blazing skyscraper, weren't disturbed. 'And I can't afford a hung-over crew. Have you forgotten all I taught you?'

'Printed on my memory in letters of fire,' Manon growled softly. 'Nip smartly aboard, cast off, coil the ropes neatly and go below to make the tea. Standard practice until I'm pregnant, I suppose?' she sniffed indignantly. 'Did you ring your place? How are the children?'

'Happily exhausted, full of plans for tomorrow and dead asleep at Henley.' His eyes smiled although the rest of his face remained expressionless. 'Battle gave them a lightning tour of London and fed them unsuitable food in a self-service place. He says they must have stomachs lined with cast-iron!'

Manon spared a second to regret her lost youth as he piloted her out of the lounge and up the stairs, but she kept her face calm.

'Toss you for first in the shower.' she suggested blithely, but her bravado took a dive as Stephan proved he could still out-think her.

'We'll share as we did before,' which reduced her performance to a pitiful travesty of a smile as she lowered her long, silky, lashes to hide the agony in her eyes. 'No need to look so tragic,' he murmured gently. 'It's all part of learning to live together again, and it needn't be half as bad as you imagine. Forget about everything else and just do what comes naturally!'

'Skewer you with a bare bodkin,' she hazarded

boldly, and watched his eyes crinkle with amusement.

'And break up an unbeatable combination?' He shook his head as he tilted her face upwards with a long finger under her chin to look down at her enigmatically. 'We only function properly when we're together!'

Afterwards, Manon lay awake for a long time in the darkness, listening to the deep, even breathing of her husband and cursing the weakness of her body. She had known she couldn't hide some things, but Stephan's practised lovemaking had stripped her of even the smallest pretence. He had encouraged her lavishly and she had gone back in time to be, once again, the eager, uninhibited, passionate girl of three years ago, responding to his smallest caress with wild abandon and only remembering afterwards that he was an inconsiderate devil who didn't mean a word of the love talk he murmured in the darkness, who had married her to get a child and who would dismiss her as soon as his object was achieved.

Her eyes filled with tears and she stirred restlessly, only to have a strong arm tighten about her naked body and draw her close so that she felt the cool dampness of his skin against hers. With a little sigh of resignation, she relaxed. There was no point in spending the rest of the night in soul-searching, she would be like a limp dishcloth when morning came.

'Tea or coffee?' Stephan woke her early with a kiss that set her pulses pounding, but this was no time to think of anything but the present. The past was dead and to think of the future would drive her crazy. He was shaved and dressed in jeans and shirt with rope-soled, canvas shoes on his feet ready for the boat. Manon envied him his compartmented mind which could shut out everything but the object of the moment. She even forgave him the quick glance at his watch. Getting the *Speedwell* to sea was uppermost in his thoughts and he wouldn't want to miss the tide.

'Coffee.' She dragged the sheet up to cover her as she sat up, and if there was a derisory twist to his mouth at her frail attempt at modesty, she pretended not to see it. 'No milk,' she added, scrabbling around for something to cover her and giving him a perfunctory nod of thanks as he fished her silk robe from where it had hidden itself under the bed. 'So it'll be cool enough to drink when I've had a shower,' she explained. 'Shan't keep you long. Are my things . . .?'

'Waiting for you on the boat, you can change when you get there.' Stephan was economical with words, his head bent as he poured coffee. 'Put a few suitable things in a suitcase, you'll need them when we go ashore,' he added.

She would dearly have liked to grab her cup and take it with her, but first things first, and pulling the robe tightly about her, she scampered off to the sound of 'Breakfast will be ready in ten minutes.'

Stephan left the Rolls in the hotel car-park, hiring a taxi to take them to Bosham, and a weatherbeaten old man rowed them out to *Speedwell* where she lay dancing at her mooring buoy and rocking to every slap of the ripples on her gleaming hull. Everything laid on, Manon told herself sardonically as she kicked off her high-heeled shoes to scramble up the ladder to the deck. Stephen was the complete and efficient manager.

While she was getting aboard and in the short time it took her to change into new stiff jeans, flannel shirt, thick sweater and soft-soled shoes, she mused on. He had taken over her life and it was now running on oiled wheels, but only where he wanted it to run, and she spared a thought as to how long it would take her to get pregnant.

She added up the pros and cons of being married to Stephan, trying to be honest with herself and came to the humiliating conclusion that life with him—now she had had a second taste of it—was infinitely preferable to life without him, and that had nothing to do with luxury living. As for her dedication to the theatre, it was now coming a poor second to life with Stephan, but she shrugged the thought aside to concentrate on her present role. There would be only a limited audience, but whenever they had one, she would give the performance of her life. The pity of it was that most of it wouldn't be acting; she would just be doing what came naturally!

Speedwell's diesel engine roared in reverse, she backed away from her mooring, and when she was clear, went quietly ahead to make a tight circle and head slowly down the creek towards the open water of Bracklesham Bay. Belatedly, Manon hauled the dripping lines aboard, coiled them neatly and then, with a grimace at Stephan's absorbed stance at the wheel, went below to the tiny galley and brewed a pot of tea.

'If you've so much money you have to employ a minder and it gives you so much trouble,' she plonked the tea-mug down where he could reach it, 'why don't you give some of it away?' she posed the question tartly. 'A million here, a million there. You'd never notice it with all those noughts after the numbers which come after the pound sign.'

'I do my best, but it's not as easy as it sounds.' Somehow the tension between them had slackened and she felt easier. It was almost as though she were young and gay again with no memories to haunt her, and she was able to respond to his gentle teasing. Out of the corner of her eye, she watched his face. It would never be naked so that she could read what he was thinking, but it seemed so much less shuttered that she listened to his explanation gravely.

'If I were ever called upon to find a really large sum at short notice, it would mean realising some assets, turning stocks and shares into cash.' He spelled it out patiently and she listened attentively. There seemed to be a lot more in this money business than she had ever imagined. 'A very tricky business,' he shrugged. 'The Stock Market might get jumpy if I started selling. Share prices are fickle things, it only needs a rumour to set them tumbling, then everybody loses.'

'I get the picture,' she grimaced distastefully. 'Then how about buying a desert island?'

'Hardly an original thought. There aren't many left.' His soft laugh took her by surprise. 'All bought up by Greek and American millionaires, and for much the same reasons.'

Manon looked around; the scene they were leaving was innocuous—a scattering of boats of all shapes and sizes, tied up to buoys well away from the fairway. There weren't many people about either. The seasonal sailors had nearly all departed, leaving their craft cocooned protectively against the coming winter. Others, the dedicated, were still working; painting, varnishing and repairing before they went ashore to their trim little houses where they would go into a state of suspended animation until spring and good sailing weather came round again.

It all seemed far away from high finance, threats and ransoms; she was in a different world, a better world where such ugliness didn't exist and the only important things were fair weather and a safe landfall at the day's end. She knew that kidnapping and extortion were common happenings nowadays, but her mind balked at the thought of it possibly happening to her or hers. This only demonstrated the huge gulf between her and Stephan, who accepted precautions as an everyday fact of life.

He however didn't seem to think that a gulf existed between them, or if it did, he had bridged it, but Manon wasn't so sanguine. A period, no matter how short, of being hedged about, guarded and protected, looked dismal. Now it had been pointed out to her, she would be in a perpetual state of worry about Harry, Fennie; about everybody.

It took the shine out of the morning and she retired gloomily to the galley with a cold, sick feeling in her stomach which wasn't caused by the motion of the boat. But with nothing much to do, the little galley soon became claustrophobic and she escaped into the saloon to throw herself on to one of the navy blue unholstered banquettes, tug a cushion beneath her cheek and close her eyes. She had slept very little last night, been woken far too early, and she was dog-tired already. It was some little time later that the note of the engine changed to a heavier throb, waking her from her doze, and she guessed they were out of the winding channel of the creek and in open water.

Time to make coffee, and when it was ready, she carried Stephan's to him at the wheel.

'Are you warm enough?' he murmured as he looked her over. 'There's a stiff breeze coming off the water and once we're round the Foreland, it'll be rough.'

'Oh!' She was flip, remembering the little bit of sailing cant she had picked up from him in what seemed another life. 'I shall stand in your lee, you're big enough to keep the wind off me!' But when she went back to the galley to inspect the provisions, her mouth tightened and her eyes were hard as she returned to the bridge.

'You must have had this in mind all along!' she accused wildly, with a mental picture of chops, sausages, bacon and eggs, canned drinks and even a couple of bottles of wine as well as the usual dry goods, bread, butter and a carton of milk. 'It looks as though you've been planning all this for months.'

'Six, to be precise. Where would I be without forethought?' Stephan gave her the glimmerings of a smile.

'You were that sure?' she marvelled ironically.

'I put a lot of work into it,' he shrugged, 'and remember, I know you very well. I know your weak spot, all I had to do was prepare the ground and throw out a life-line when you were going under for the third time. You had to accept, Manon, you had no alternative.'

His calm aggravated her rage. 'My baby died because of an accident and you've treated me as though I were a murderess! You've hounded me, ruined my career, deprived me of a living!' She became careless of what she said. After all, what further harm could he do her? Physical violence wasn't in his line. 'So, if you've been so damned beforehand with your preparations,' she continued acidly, seizing on the least little thing which annoyed her and magnifying it out of all proportion, 'why didn't you lay in more milk? One carton's not going to last long and I loathe the powdered stuff in tea. What's the wine for anyway? Loving toasts? I want out of all this togetherness!'

'We get fresh milk ashore every evening when we tie up somewhere, and you revel in the togetherness, although you prefer to pretend.' She sensed his patience was wearing thin, but she didn't care. She had been forced into this and she was determined to make him regret it even if she hurt herself doing so. She had little control over the nights, but she would make the days uncomfortable.

Nevertheless, this first day passed without any real trouble. Manon, with nothing much to do, shrugged herself into the oilskin jacket Stephan had thoughtfully provided, extinguished the dark fire of her hair with a thick woolly hat which she pulled down well over her ears and came up on deck to watch the coastline slide past. Stephan obviously wasn't in a hurry, *Speedwell* slipped along easily, her bows creaming through the green waves and her wake spreading out behind her like a peacock's tail. Past the Foreland, the muted throb of the engines developed into a healthy roar and Manon leant against the guard rails with salt spray battering her face as first Shanklin then Ventnor receded and they were rounding St Catherine's Point into Brighstone Bay.

The sight of Swanage and Lulworth with the Durdle Door standing out like part of some prehistoric building brought back bittersweet memories. Stephan had taken her there, saying there was nowhere more beautiful than the Dorset coast, but that had been more than three years ago. It had been spring and her love had been fresh and sparkling with no tawdriness to smear it into the ugly, shameful thing it had become later. With a sigh, she left the rail and went below to make lunch, making herself busy so that memory wouldn't hurt so much, and by the time the soup was hot and the rest of the meal ready, they were well into Weymouth Bay.

'Soup and hamburgers,' she announced as she brought Stephan his share. 'I haven't found my way round the provisions yet.' She cast a curious eye at the chart table. The pencilled lines were dark and definite, but they bypassed Weymouth and she raised her eyebrows. 'I thought we might be stopping at Wey . . .?'

'We've made good time,' Stephan shrugged. 'I'd like to get as far as possible while the weather holds. Besides, Weymouth's pretty busy now, I thought we'd do better at Lyme Regis or West Bay. Any preference, Manon?'

'No.' she shrugged unco-operatively, setting the food down just where he could reach it. 'I'm only the crew and as far as I'm concerned, either will do as long as we can get some fresh milk. We'll need some for breakfast tomorrow morning.'

Afterwards, she sat below, chewing and listening

to the mewing of the gulls. They only came when there was food about, which meant that Stephan was up to his old tricks. He hated hamburgers, he only ever ate the meat. He threw the bun overboard!

CHAPTER FIVE

WHEN the business of finding their mooring and tying up was completed, Manon struggled out of salt-sticky clothes, showered, slipped into clean underwear and inspected her reflection carefully. She had the white skin that went with her hair colour and her eyes, a difficult skin which never tanned properly, and already she could see the beginnings of a good crop of freckles across the bridge of her nose. She made a disgusted sound in her throat which was answered by Stephan's amused chuckle as he squeezed into the small toilet compartment behind her and looked over her shoulder.

'I like them,' he murmured, turning her to face him and touching the faint spray of brown flecks with a long finger. She flinched away from him, but there wasn't enough room to put any real distance between them. The jutting curve of the wash-basin rammed into the small of her back and the shower stall on one side and the loo on the other prevented any sideways movement, so she stood very still and shivered as she felt his arms slide about her.

'They make you look human,' he continued reflectively. 'I don't care for the porcelain-doll image.'

'Please!' The involuntary protest broke from her lips, but as she heard the hoarse little sound, she knew it was useless. She could feel him pressing against her, hard and masculine; feel her own avid response and was ashamed by its eagerness. 'I have to dress, go ashore and find a chemist,' she babbled. 'I need . . .'

'Mmm.' His hand drifted down to touch the pale green silk that covered her breast, 'I know exactly what you need, you're one of the most transparent women I've ever known. Your inability to hide your feelings used to be your greatest charm, but you've grown another skin while we've been apart. You're not so transparent now. That morning you came to the hotel, you had me foxed for a while. I kept wondering what had happened to my Manon.'

'Your Manon!' She raised a derisive eyebrow and stiffened in his arm. 'Your Manon grew up,' she told him flatly. 'Motherhood has that effect, you know—one matures. And now, if you don't mind I'd like to finish dressing. I need some cream for my face. That's all I want for the present, thank you!'

'Nothing else?' Stephan's mouth curved into a mocking smile and she lifted her chin. She also relaxed and stopped trying to hide her half-nude self behind her hands, letting them fall to her side while her eyes hardened with the effort she was putting into preserving a cool exterior.

'I can't think of a thing,' she retorted, 'unless you'd be good enough to pass me that towelling wrap hanging behind the door. It's not exactly midsummer and you're nearer to it than I am.'

'Anything to oblige!' The wrap was dropped over her shoulders. Stephan didn't waste words and his movements were so well co-ordinated that she blinked at the speed with which he moved. The wrap was about her and he had gone before she had time to say another word, but she shouted a sardonic 'Thank you' as the door of the toilet compartment closed behind him.

The old port of West Bay had changed very little in the three years since Manon had last seen it. The great sandstone cliffs were dramatic as ever and it was still a Mecca for fishermen and the sailing fraternity. The two beaches were good for bathing, and from the deck of the *Speedwell*, Manon could make out the cottages and the old slate-hung Customs House which fringed one beach; but which one it was, not being either a swimmer or a sunbather, she couldn't remember.

Speedwell was tied up to a buoy offshore and when Manon stepped out on to the harbour wall from the inflatable dinghy, she gave Stephan a killing look.

'I shall need some money,' she told him flatly. 'I can hardly pay for a bottle of sun-lotion with a cheque. I shall come back to meet you later,' she added bitterly, 'so you needn't be afraid of my running away or disappearing from the face of the earth because you've given me a bit of cash!'

'Of course you'd come back.' Nothing, not her bad temper nor her lack of co-operation, seemed to affect Stephan; he just ignored it. 'You're secretive but not dishonest. You've given your word and that's good enough for me. However, I'll come with you and when you've bought whatever it is you require, we'll find a place for a meal.'

'Fed up with my cooking already?' she jeered, but

it slid off him like water from a duck's back as he tied up the small craft and clambered ashore to join her. It was as though he weren't listening, and almost at once, before the humour of this ridiculous situation struck her, Manon started to feel mean and petty. Here she was, married to the only man she had ever loved or wanted to marry. It mightn't be exactly how she wanted it, but it was better than nothing. She should be trying to forget the past and concentrate on the present; be an adult and build herself some good memories to live on when she was once more alone. Very few people were completely happy, life didn't seem to work that way.

'Sorry, I'm being bitchy.' Her rueful apology brought his infrequent smile to curve his mouth. 'It's just that things have happened so swiftly,' she excused herself breathily; she was almost having to run to keep up with his long strides as they left the sea wall and headed into the town.

'You're possibly a bit disorientated,' he shrugged. 'It seems to be taking you a long time to adjust, but this isn't a game we're playing. I know I've rushed you, but you should accept instead of showing your claws and spitting at every opportunity. I told you, we both have things to forgive and be forgiven, so shall we call a truce?' His nose lifted and he looked down at her with a wary look in his dark eyes. 'I find this constant bickering very tiresome,' he added flatly.

He had stopped outside a chemist's shop and was peering in the window. 'Can you get what you want here?'

'Oh, yes.' Her eyes travelled over a display of her

favourite toiletries and the smile that tugged at her lips was one of wry anticipation. 'Adjustment's only a frame of mind dictated by circumstances, and since the circumstances are so good, I think I'll have the lot. Bath-salts, soaps, creams, shampoo, make-up, perfume. That's if you think the labourer worthy of her hire?'

'Worth every penny as long as you go easy with the stuff while we're on board.' Stephan slid an arm about her shoulders and turned her to face him. 'You always smell delightful, but in a confined space . . .!'

'A genuine compliment at last!' and there was no fake about her involuntary chuckle, it had an amused ring. 'But as you suggest, I won't be too liberal or you'll be rushing up on deck for a breath of fresh air.'

They dined very well among a crowd of other nautical types at a small hotel where the food was good and plentiful, the vegetables hadn't been frozen and the trifle for dessert contained so much sherry and was covered by so thick a layer of cream that Manon felt guilty as she accepted a second helping. But the sea air had made her hungry and she realised that she hadn't been truly hungry for a long time. She bit into a brandy-soaked cherry and stopped worrying about her weight. She was too thin anyway, she could afford to put on a couple of pounds!

It was quite dark when she stepped down into the dinghy, still clasping her precious carrier bag of toiletries and basking in a lovely full-fed feeling of content. She hugged her boat-jacket about her against the night chill and trailed her fingers to make phosphorescent streaks in the dark water which felt so much warmer than the air as the little outboard motor chugged them sturdily towards *Speedwell*, a dim white shape rolling gently at her mooring.

With any luck, if she did as Stephan suggested and stopped fighting, she could make this period of obligation tolerable, an amnesty. She couldn't hope for the kind of relationship they had had before, that would be too much to expect, with the bitter memories which lay between them and the thought of the equally bitter, lonely future ahead for her, but there could be something, a working arrangement where she wouldn't be hurt too much.

'Pax,' she agreed belatedly, watching as he climbed the stern ladder after her and stepped on to the deck.

'You mean that?' She could hardly see his face in the darkness, but his voice was quiet and almost understanding. 'You won't fight any more?'

'That would be asking a bit too much,' she reproved him, but not nastily. 'I've a mind of my own. Let's just say I'll work at it and try to earn my pay.'

'Mmm.' His arm slid about her shoulders and drew her close so that she had the scent of him in her nostrils; a dry, very clean scent and a seductive warmth which made her slightly dizzy. 'As of now?' The question was no more than a murmur in her ear.

'As of now,' she nodded, and then remembered something important. 'Oh hell, I forgot the milk!'

Next morning, a touch on her shoulder and the smell of frying bacon wakened her and she rolled over on to her back, opening her eyes regretfully. It had been a lovely dream, she had been happy, she couldn't remember what it had been about, but now she was back to the 'life is real, life is earnest' thing of everyday living, and Stephan was wafting the steam from a cup of coffee towards her nose.

'Wake up, sleepyhead,' he ordered crisply. 'Breakfast is ready. I've been ashore, fetched the milk and hoisted the dinghy back aboard. The weather forecast's good and I'd like to get under way as soon as possible. With any luck, we'll make the French coast before dark.'

But the Channel was living up to its reputation for being unpredictable. Despite a blue sky and a sun which was quite warm, away from the shelter of the coast the wind was almost gale force and the sea was rough with big rolling waves which tossed *Speedwell* about as if she were of no more consequence than the dinghy.

Stephan slid a glance at Manon's face as she clung to the chart-table for support. 'Not feeling sick, are you?'

'N-no,' she gasped ruefully, and blenched as the bows dipped and another wave broke against them to send spray hurtling against the windscreen, blotting out the heaving sea until the wipers cleared it to show another white-crested wave swooping down on them. 'Just scared to death, that's all!'

'You'd be better below, in the saloon,' he advised. 'If rough weather frightens you, this is the worst place to be. I forgot you've only stooged around in coastal waters so far.'

'Thanks, but no.' Hastily, she switched her gaze to a side window from which she could still see the coastline of England. She didn't feel so frightened with land in sight, but soon it would be out of sight and she didn't want to be alone. Besides, there was something very comforting about Stephan's imperturbability, it gave her confidence. 'I'd rather stay with you, if you don't mind.'

Speedwell gave a sideways lurch that sent her sprawling against him and she was grateful for the strength of the arm which caught and held her, although his sardonic chuckle made her mad.

'Any port in a storm—even me, Manon? What's happened to your cherished independence?'

Manon recovered herself briskly, 'In these conditions, any port, damn you!' She stressed the 'any'. 'If you were a grizzly bear, I'd be hanging on to your fur!'

The rough seas slowed them up and Stephan, with one eye on the fuel gauge—with full tanks and smooth running, *Speedwell* could notch up about two hundred miles—decided to make for Jersey. The wind was still strong, Manon was a trifle green, but as they passed the Corbière lighthouse where the waves were pounding so hard the rocks couldn't be seen for spray, Stephan shouted at her encouragingly.

'Here, it's only really rough when the waves go right over the top of the lighthouse.'

They tied up close to the refuelling point in St Helier, alongside another motor cruiser undergoing a refit. It was the only sheltered berth available, and they set about getting the boat snugged down for the night, after which they showered, dressed and went ashore to a small hotel for a meal and beds which stayed all in one plane.

'You need it,' Stephan told Manon. 'I'm all right, but you were beginning to look like a green drowned rat.'

'Oh, you!' She heaved an outraged sigh. 'There's no getting the better of you, is there?'

'No.' This time, his smile expanded while his heavy lids and long lashes hid his eyes. 'Not you, Manon. I can beat you any time. As I told you yesterday, you're honest, and that makes you vulnerable.'

'And you don't suffer from that complaint?'

'I'm as honest as circumstances allow,' he said seriously. 'And as vulnerable as most men, I suppose. Tell me, Manon—except for once when, as you said, I lied by default, have I ever been dishonest with you?'

'We-ell,' she hesitated over it, 'I've noticed you don't always tell all the truth. You tend to emphasise the sugar-coating and only after I've swallowed the pill do I discover how bitter it is. But you aren't vulnerable at any point, which puts me at a disadvantage because I am,' she complained.

His infrequent laugh rang out, and he swept his arm about her slender shoulders in an intimate hug. 'If I were, my dear, I'd be very careful to hide it from you. You'd be much too quick at sticking the knife in if you thought you'd found a weak spot!'

It was a very superior small hotel, and after bouncing on her choice of the twin beds, Manon bathed, changed and went down to eat an excellent dinner. Somehow, the rough passage had eased her relationship with her husband and she wasn't having to act at all. A lot of the dull despair which had filled her had vanished and she was beginning to relax. Three years of hard work plus six months of worrying were retreating into the haze which was yesterday, while thinking about the future was too harrowing and she determined not to do it.

When dinner was over, Stephan spent nearly half an hour on the phone to Battle, listening to a progress report and issuing instructions—she assumed—but she didn't wait up for him. The fresh air, the good food and a couple of glasses of wine had made her sleepy and she was just dozing off when he entered the bedroom. There were the quiet sounds as he moved about, undressing, the soft hiss of the shower and then the creak as her bed took the strain of the extra weight.

'You've got your own bed,' she grumbled sleepily, but then his arms were about her and his mouth on hers, silencing her grumbles, and she sighed for her weakness. She never had refused him, and never would be able to.

'I'm old-fashioned, I share with my wife,' murmured Stephan against her lips, 'single or king-size. You're good in bed, my dear. I've never met anybody better.'

'Another compliment, and not one I really care for,' she sighed, and gave herself up to the magic their bodies made together.

In the morning, Stephan saw to topping up the fuel

tanks before they left, and since it was only a short trip to the Brittany coast they arrived at Dinard early in the afternoon. A resort especially for the English, it had a cosmopolitan atmosphere, but Manon enjoyed it. On their walk about that evening, she singled out what she decided were the real Breton French restaurants and made sure she knew where to find them again. What was the use of being in France and eating food cooked in the English way?

On the second day of their stay, she made a pig of herself dining on a Breton dish, lobster *à l'armoricaine*, before she and Stephan wandered into one of the two casinos. To her, gambling seemed a waste of time and money, but it would be a new experience, so she accepted the pile of plastic chips Stephan bought for her, to stand, merely watching the other players' expressions while she tried to make sense of the game.

A loud burst of laughter, high and excited, drew her attention and she looked up at the loud talking group on the other side of the roulette wheel. Not a group of ordinary tourists, she decided, mentally pricing the women's clothes and jewellery. The upper crust out on a bender, getting their hand in before they started on the serious business of enjoying themselves at Monte Carlo. One voice rose clearly above the others, and she stiffened involuntarily as memory came rushing back.

'Darling,' it said, 'I've won!' The woman raised her sleek blonde head and her blue eyes met Manon's across the breadth of the table; met and held her gaze while, for Manon, everything became very quiet like an old-fashioned silent movie. Her heart beat quickened and she heard the thunder of blood in her ears; so loud she could hear nothing else.

She was back three years in time, sitting in *Speedwell's* saloon, while this same blonde's voice was saying vile things she could never forget, reducing her wonderful love to gutter level. The counters fell on to the table from her nerveless fingers and she wanted desperately to run away, put as great a distance as possible between herself and the first Mrs Vestris, but she couldn't move.

'Faites vos jeux, mesdames, messieurs . . . Rien ne va plus.' Gradually Manon's heart stopped its heavy throbbing and voices started to percolate; the croupier's quiet chant, excited speculation from the other players, and then another silence fell, but still Manon couldn't look away from those blue eyes. The wheel spun, she could hear the rattle of the ball as it ran, but these were just sounds, they didn't mean anything until the blonde's voice came again.

'And now I've lost everything and you've won!' Manon found herself flinching away from the threat that lay beneath the congratulatory words and the vicious intensity of the blue eyes which were now looking, not at her but over her shoulder. Play forgotten, she took a step backwards, only to come up against the bulk of Stephan's seemingly immovable body, and heard his voice in her ear.

'Bored with it, Manon? Pick up your chips and we'll go. It's always wiser to quit while you're ahead.' She looked down at the table to see the croupier's rake pushing a small pile of plastic towards her, but she had the oddest idea that neither Stephan nor his ex-wife had really spoken to her at all, she had no real part in whatever it was between these two, and whatever it was, it wasn't nice. They seemed to be almost threatening each other. She took a deep breath, surprised that after such a shock she should feel so normal, and turned a wry smile on him.

'Beginner's luck,' she shrugged. 'It may never happen again, so I'll take your advice,' and she was rewarded by an enigmatic look from his dark eyes which did nothing to straighten out the confusion in her mind.

'You want a drink before bed?' They were back aboard *Speedwell* and Stephan was eyeing her speculatively, as if she were a cat and he wasn't sure which way she would jump. He hadn't mentioned the encounter with his ex and she had promised herself she wouldn't speak about it until he did. Maybe then, she would learn the woman's name. She realised muzzily that Stephan had never mentioned it.

'No, I don't think so.' She complimented herself on another bit of good acting, even her yawn was just right, unstudied and convincing. 'Did I win a fortune? No, don't tell me. I can hardly keep my eyes open. I'm for bed, I feel a bit odd. I don't think I'll even bother about a shower, G'night, see you in the morning.' And with a vague wave of her hand and another stifled yawn she drifted past him, out of the saloon and into the cabin where she contemplated the bed which appeared to be heaving up and down in a very sick-making fashion.

Shock, she told herself muzzily, and then put her hand to her stomach as an excruciating pain shot through her, making her cold forehead bead with perspiration. Not shock, she decided, but lobster, she could taste it at the back of her throat, and hurriedly she dived for the toilet compartment, where suddenly her blue-eyed predecessor became an unimportant cog in the scheme of things.

Another violent pain knifed through her: bile, sour and horrid, rose in her throat and as the walls started a slow majestic dance and the low ceiling tilted at a fantastic angle she gave a weak cry for help while she clung to the basin for support.

Sick as she was, she could still feel embarrassment at being found in such a condition, so that when she felt Stephan's arm about her and the support of his hand on her cold, wet forehead she tried to fight him off, but all the strength had gone from her limbs. When the final spasm of sickness had passed, she closed her eyes and slumped against him, too weak to protest as he cleaned her up. His hands were gentle as they wielded the damp sponge and his arms a comfort so that she was almost grateful.

'You feel better now?' The jumble of words she had been hearing started to make sense and Manon opened her eyes. She was lying on one of the banquettes in the saloon, covered with a rough blue blanket and feeling cold but clean and nearly empty. Her teeth chattered as she tried to thank him through the brandy he was dribbling into her mouth; tears of humiliation rolled down her cheeks and she groped for his hand and clung to it as though it were a lifeline.

She had never felt so ill in all her life, not even after she had lost the baby, and she was grateful when he pulled another blanket out from its hidey-hole, kicked off his shoes and lay down beside her, drawing the blankets up to cover them both and gathering her close against the warmth of his body.

'We don't have a hot-water bottle aboard.' His voice came as a breath of sound in her ears. 'Can you make do with me? And stop feeling guilty. That lobster's a well-known tourist trap and you must have been living on a starvation diet for months.'

'And whose fault is that?' she groaned, not bothering to deny it. 'Who fixed it so I couldn't afford to eat?' She turned her head away and blinked on more tears. In between the bouts of pain and sickness, her mind was working again. Because of her, Manon Lucas, a marriage had been broken up and Fennie was motherless. Her wonderful love hadn't been so wonderful after all. Love didn't go around hurting other people, or it shouldn't. She closed her eyes, shutting out the sight of Stephan as another wave of shame and self-reproach added itself to the sickness and made her cringe.

'I don't need a lecture,' she moaned. 'Go away, leave me alone. I just want to die!'

But he didn't go, he stayed, dribbling more brandy between her lips, fetching a nauseous dose from the medicine cabinet and forcing her to drink it and then holding her until she fell into an uneasy sleep.

Things didn't look any better in the morning. She

had spent a hideous night, alternating between
bouts of nausea and periods of recollection that had
made her sweat with self-disgust and humiliation.
Her pride was in rags, and she struggled up on deck
with a greenish tinge to her complexion and a
stomach that kept turning somersaults.

Stephan shook his head at her sadly with an 'I
told you so' expression, folded up the upholstered
seat beside his own which allowed her to sit beside
him while he steered from the bridge and sent her
back to the saloon where she arranged herself, flat
on her back, praying alternately for either death,
firm ground beneath her feet or that she'd never
been born at all.

But what had happened had happened, and
though she regretted it, she couldn't change it. She
had never meant to hurt anybody and now she must
live with it. She had given her word, made her
bargain and taken her pay, so this charade would
have to go on. It hadn't been too bad so far, she had
established a tolerable relationship with Stephan
and she didn't have to understand the way his mind
worked. He wasn't paying for understanding and
she didn't want to understand.

There must be a wide gulf between the sexes, else
how could a man live with a woman and make crazy
love to her when he was only using her? Only a
certain type of man could do a thing like that, one
with no real emotion and no commitment. Perhaps
it was the nausea, but suddenly the whole relationship between them seemed ugly, intolerable.
Manon could hardly believe she was a willing party
to it.

The crackle of the radio disturbed her and the turmoil in her stomach suddenly increased. While they were aboard, the only person who called was Battle—on a regular basis, every evening. Stephan had said this was standard practice—but this was morning, so it was something different. She glanced at her watch, only ten o'clock, and a call at this hour seemed to have an almost ominous significance. The radio crackle sounded again and she dragged herself from the banquette and on to the bridge with a black premonition enhancing the curdle of sickness.

By the time she reached the bridge, the call was finished and Stephan was removing his headphones. That also was significant, Battle's voice was always plainly audible through the receiver, so Stephan must have plugged in the headphones. It was obviously something he hadn't wanted her to hear, and she leaned against the door jamb watching as he started to plot out a new course at the chart table, and when that was done, he reached for the log book.

Manon knew what that meant. Stephan was meticulous about the log, every change of course, every departure and arrival was logged automatically, so he must be intending to leave Dinard. That wasn't what she had understood, he had told her they were to stay for another day at least.

Since she had missed the conversation, she carefully examined his face, but it was as closed and expressionless as ever. Too expressionless, she decided, and another glance at the chart showed a pencilled line crossing the Channel to England.

Whatever the message had been, it must have been important to be taking them back to England without delay. All her fears multiplied until they settled in a tight knot in her stomach where they set up a violent reaction with the effects of the lobster, making her mouth go dry and her headache increase.

'What's the matter?' she demanded weakly as she slumped against the door. The boat was rocking slightly and her face took on a greener tinge. 'Who was that calling?' Her mind had leapt to Harry, although she spared a thought for little Fennie.

'Battle,' Stephan said calmly. 'No sweat, but we have to go back at once. D'you feel up to making coffee while I get ready to cast off?'

'Harry's all right?' she demanded hysterically, 'and Fennie? Nothing's happened to them? You're sure?'

'Of course I'm sure. This is business, Manon—a merger I've been working on, nothing to do with the children, so go and make the coffee like a good girl; you'll feel better having something to do.'

By the time all the formalities were completed and extra fuel taken aboard, they were late leaving Dinard, but Stephan made up lost time on the crossing. Fortunately, this time the Channel was as smooth as a millpond and *Speedwell* cut her way through the slight swell at a speed which Manon thought frightening, but once they were in sight of England, a lot of the dash vanished in the fight against currents and the ebb tide, and she ground her teeth with impatience as Stephan throttled back and stooged around, waiting for slack water before he entered Bosham creek.

The armorican lobster with its over-rich brown sauce of tomatoes, shallots, garlic and brandy had ceased to trouble her, only a gnawing emptiness remained, but to be on the safe side she hadn't eaten any of the sandwiches she had made to go with the constant supply of coffee and hot soup she had provided all the way across the Channel.

It was nearly dark when the same old weather-beaten boatman came out to row them ashore, hardly making a ripple or a splash on the dark, smooth water of the creek, and Manon, whose thoughts had become gloomy once more, found herself thinking of Charon rowing his boat of the dead across the Styx. Would they be landing at the Elysian Fields or would she find herself somewhere less pleasant? In the rapidly fading light, she watched as Stephan reached for his wallet, and when some notes had changed hands, some superstitious instinct made her thrust a handful of loose change into the old man's gnarled fingers. It was all she had in the world and it was as though she had been carrying it around all this time for just this purpose. One should always pay the ferryman!

CHAPTER SIX

THERE was a taxi waiting and after a swift visit to the hotel in Chichester to pick up the car, Manon, still in salt-stained jeans, shirt and boat-jacket, found herself in the comfort of the Rolls and speeding Londonwards, to what? Stephan broke the long silence between them.

'Sorry about this early return, my dear. We'd hardly begun to pick up the pieces.'

'Pick up as many pieces as you like,' she heard herself sounding surly. 'You can't stick them back together again, there's no glue strong enough for that!'

'I thought we were doing a good reconstruction job.' The dim glow from the dashboard showed her a smiling but enigmatic profile, but it was only half a page which she couldn't read. She needed him full face so that she could make a guess at what was going on behind his eyes. 'There's been nothing wrong with the nights,' he continued blandly, 'and I thought the days were becoming more tolerable.'

'I don't think we need produce anything more substantial than a façade,' she ground out between clenched teeth, glad of the darkness to hide the hot colour in her face. 'It's not as though we were contemplating anything lasting!' Saying it gave her pleasure and pain, both at the same time, so that she didn't know whether to laugh or cry. But it was better to keep reminding herself that all this would end some time. That way, she wouldn't be living in a fool's paradise or dreaming impossible dreams. So she closed her eyes and lapsed into a silence so thick and heavy that it stifled her.

'The London hotel?' She spoke when she couldn't stand the silence any longer.

'No, Henley,' Stephan put her right without wasting words. 'We're going home, Manon.'

'Home?' Tiredness was overwhelming her and she hardly knew what she was saying. Her eyes closed and she could hear her voice slurring as talking became too much of an effort.

Much later, a feeling of motionlessness woke her. It was quite dark and she stirred in her seat and looked out through the windscreen into blackness pierced by the headlights shining on closed iron gates. But she came to life refreshed by her sleep, with a stomach which no longer revolted at the thought of food. Indeed, it was clamouring for something to fill its emptiness.

'Worse than Fort Knox!' she exclaimed derisively. 'Ring twice and give the password. Oh lord! Will you look at that!' as Battle came marching down the drive to open the gates. 'All done by mirrors?'

'Closed circuit TV,' Stephan corrected her as he acknowledged Battle's para-military salute, a definite 'thumbs up' sign, and drove slowly through the opened gates and even more slowly up the drive. 'The gates are locked after dark and there's a camera nearby with some infra-red gear so Battle can see who's calling.'

Manon sniffed. 'I wonder anybody does! What comes next, I wonder? A ringing of bells, trip-wires and landmines? Why couldn't you have been a pauper and lived in a cottage?'

Stephan brought the car to a halt by the steps up

to the house and switched off the engine, but he made no move towards the switch that controlled the central door-locking. Instead, he turned to her, his face illuminated only by the reflected glow of the headlights.

'You'd prefer to live in a cottage with a pauper, Manon?'

'It'd help,' she shrugged, stifling the impulse to tell him she would live in a tent if he would share it with her and tell her, just once, that he loved her. 'This way, I'm getting a taste for luxury. I'll come down to earth with an almighty bump when you no longer require my services.'

'"For as long as it takes",' he reminded her. 'After that, you can have anything you want, although I can't guarantee to provide the pauper.'

'Promises, promises,' she sighed as the car door opened smoothly and Battle was there to help her out and make his report at the same time.

'Everything quiet?' asked Stephan as he slid out of the driving-seat and tossed Battle the car keys.

'Like a graveyard except for the phone, sir. That's been working overtime.' Battle led them into the house, locked and bolted the door after them, slid into the 'at ease' position and made sucking noises between his teeth. 'Sorry to have mucked up your arrangements, but your Mr Preston was insistent. He's sent a messenger down with all the relevant info—I've put the briefcase in your study—and he asked me to pass on a message . . .' Battle tapered off to a halt while he arranged and rearranged his words. Manon could almost see him doing it and it needed Stephan's sharp 'What messsage?' to start him off again.

'Er . . . it's a matter of timing, sir. He's sorry to

break in on anything, but if you could go over the papers ... he'll need your signature as soon as possible—tomorrow, if that's convenient.' Duty done, Battle beamed at them both. 'Hope you had a good crossing. Miss Fennie's been a bit down— lonely, I expect, after we took young Harry back to school, but her terrier's had three pups and that cheered her up. She meant to wait up for you, but she was dropping off over her supper, so I sent her off to bed. No visitors except the vet.'

Stephan invited Manon to share the shower in their private bathroom—he said it would save time—but she refused, saying she preferred a bath. Unreasonably shy after nearly five days of very close contact, she also refused to share that with him, although the tub was huge.

'So much modesty,' he mocked. 'Isn't it a bit late for that—three years too late?'

'Never too late.' Although she was tired and hungry, Manon still had enough life left in her to put up the necessary fight against herself. 'And you would bring that up, wouldn't you? But so what? Am I going to have it thrown in my face every time I won't do exactly what you want? I admit that even three years ago I was old enough to know better, but I didn't have any experience, and nobody knows that better than you do! Compared with yours, my past is as pure as driven snow,' she continued, not shouting but dropping each word clearly and weightily, although her voice had risen to a high note.

'I'm not throwing anything in your face,' he denied quietly. 'I'm just reminding you ...'

'You're rubbing my nose in it!' she squealed irritably. 'Just because I feel like a bit of privacy for a change! After a few days alone with you on a little boat, I'm fed up with all this togetherness.' There was a small, velvet-upholstered armchair in the window bay and she seated herself in it firmly, trying to look like an immovable object.

'There's no privacy in marriage,' he pointed out gravely, but she was in no mood to be reasonable.

'There's going to be, in this one!' She snorted with temper. 'I've been down-graded to the level of a brood mare. You've hardly left me with a shred of self-respect, and all the money in the world, all the classy clothes, even a temporary home won't give that back to me. I won't have the past resurrected every time I do or say something you don't approve of, and I insist on some privacy!'

There was a cliff-hanger of a pause as Stephan stood and just looked at her. She watched his nostrils pinch and his mouth become a straight line. Was this another of his faces? If so, she didn't like it, it frightened her, as did his hands when they grasped her shoulders and hauled her out of the chair. There was neither kindness or gentleness in his grip, his fingers pressed painfully, squeezing through her skin and the thin layer of flesh which covered her shoulders to press against the fine bones beneath.

'You are in no position to insist about anything.' The coldness of his voice chilled her and she could feel her fear growing like a weed until it filled her, but she kept her chin up and stared him out.

'All right!' She choked back hot words and sought swiftly for some sanity. 'I won't insist, I'll just request.'

Dark, unfathomable eyes looked deep into her own, she felt the grip loosen on her shoulders and caught the beginnings of a smile about his firm mouth.

'Request granted, Mrs Vestris. Give me five minutes to shower and you can have the bathroom to yourself while I get our supper.'

'*You* get the supper?' Her eyebrows nearly met her hairline and all her self-pity was swallowed in surprise. 'Who usually gets the meals in this house?'

'You'll be taking over the kitchen, I hope.' He had eyed her sardonically. 'We have a daily woman who comes in to clean, but our cook-housekeeper retired as soon as I told her I was getting married—said she couldn't abide working for women. Finding another at such short notice has proved unsuccessful. Can you cook, or are your talents strictly confined to the stage?'

Manon flushed and then paled with anger and her pretence of civilised behaviour fell away like a discarded cloak. 'You're doing it again!' she accused. 'Insults by implication, nasty little digs at me. I have talents in lots of areas.' She ground out the words from between clenched teeth and lips stiff with anger. 'Some, I bet you've never even thought of, though I can't match you for bedroom performance, of course! Your track-record, which I had from an unimpeachable source, would take some beating. Go boil your head and leave me alone!'

This seemed to amuse him. 'My ex-wife being your unimpeachable source, I suppose? But that was a long time ago, Manon, and haven't you considered her point of view might have been biased?'

'With cause, I dare say,' she shrugged. 'But there's no smoke without fire, and leopards don't change their spots!' and she lay back in the chair, closed her eyes and pretended she was alone.

'No leopard.' His murmur pierced through her pretence. 'Just a cosy kitchen cat.'

'A randy old tom,' she corrected briefly without opening her eyes, and went back to pretending. It was a very successful pretence, she didn't hear him go into the bathroom, but then he moved so quietly and with so little fuss, she doubted if she would have heard him in any case.

Half an hour later, driven by hunger, she made her way downstairs and into the kitchen. She had used nearly twenty-five minutes to bathe, rinsing and re-rinsing herself and her hair until not a trace of salt remained; leaving herself very little time to dress. Hastily, she had scrambled herself into a tweed skirt and an emerald green jumper—clothes of Stephan's providing, which made her feel under an obligation—and her hair, still damp, was tied back with a scrap of green ribbon. Her face was as God had made it, without a trace of make-up, deliberately so.

The total effect was far from glamourous, but she no longer cared. If there had been a penitent's sackcloth and ashes handy, she would have worn the sackcloth and smeared ash all over her face. Losing her temper and saying spiteful, savage things, even in private, showed a lack of control. It diminished her in her own eyes to an undisciplined child.

Maybe Stephan was to blame for the position she was in, but she had made a bargain with him, and being bitter and spiteful wouldn't help her to keep her side of it. She ought to act happily married even when they were alone, the practice would be good for her, and she would be able to give a better performance if ever there were an audience!

The thought of Fennie trickled into her mind; it was a sure thing that his daughter would be watching her carefully, and that would be an audience she didn't relish. Children had an uncanny ability to pick up the undercurrents. Manon recalled her own childhood and how often she had worried when her parents had squabbled in her hearing.

In the kitchen, which felt gloriously warm to her rather chilled body, the table in the breakfast area was set for two and Stephan, with swift, economic movements, was removing hot dishes from the oven on to the counter. Manon maintained a careful silence while she tried to think of something innocuous to say, something which wouldn't start another quarrel. Hadn't he shown her just how far he would go to revenge a fancied insult, waiting and plotting for three years until she was in just the position he wanted?

He had admitted that, but still she could hardly believe it. She went on watching him in silence while her stomach squeezed a protest at its emptiness and the cooking smells made her mouth water.

'I thought you didn't have a cook.' It was something to say and she waited to see how he would take it. Surprisingly—to her—he smiled.

'We don't, but we have Battle. He's very diverse, seems to be able to turn his hand to anything.'

'Most old soldiers are,' she murmured. 'Survival's the name of the game.' As she said it, she realised it applied to herself. She also had to survive, and she wouldn't do that by wearing herself out in a fight she couldn't win. 'Nice chops,' she remarked casually as he carried the dish to the table. 'I'll take over the commissariat and relieve Battle in that area—give him more time for his dog and other security measures.'

'Thank you.' She wondered if she had imagined the slight twist of humour about his mouth. 'I was hoping you'd offer. Only the food though, I'll see to the wines.'

'Mmm,' she helped herself generously from the various dishes and sighed with satisfaction as she eyed her loaded plate. 'That would be a great help,' she said sedately. 'I know nothing about wine, only that the sweet stuff gives you a headache. There's a lot of mystique about it! Château-bottled, Appellation Controllée, which with what—I'd be bound to get it wrong.'

Manon woke as dawn was breaking in a grey misty light which hardly penetrated the gauzy ruffles of the curtains. But there was light enough to see Stephan's face, dark against the whiteness of the pillows, and moving herself stealthily so as not to disturb the arm that held her, she turned to examine her husband's sleeping features.

It was a good face, at least it was while he was asleep. All the shuttering was gone and he looked much younger than his thirty-seven years, even a little bit vulnerable. As if he knew in his sleep that he was being examined, his eyes opened, and for a fraction of a second the youth and the vulnerability remained while his mouth curved into a smile and then, like a curtain falling, it was gone; replaced with his habitual impassive expression.

'You feel less evil-tempered this morning?' His arm tightened about her, drawing her closer, and she didn't protest. Some of the three-year-old magic stayed with her, of the short time when she had been so happy with him, the time before the rot set in. Then, it had been more than a mere physical attraction. She had had no qualms then, no feeling of guilt, it had seemed so inevitable, so right; as if they were two halves who needed to be together to be a complete whole, and a little voice in her mind said clearly, 'And you still do!'

She tried to ignore that voice, but it refused to be ignored. There was so much more than a three-year-old affair which bound her to Stephan. There were her memories of how it had been, of how words hadn't been important, and most of all, there had been her pitiful little child. Something of his, a part of him, but even the child had been lost to her.

'Sad thoughts?' His finger drifted across her cheek, wiping away tears she hadn't realised she was shedding.

'Life's grim.' Manon tried for a sophisticated approach, meaning it to be a throwaway remark, even wittily sardonic, but it came out sad. 'I feel definitely battered and about a hundred years old.'

'Too much lobster, too much rush. You'll feel better in the morning.' His arm was firm about her and, rather than destroy something lovely she felt was building, she rested her cheek on his chest, feeling the springy growth of hair tickle her nose and the thud of his heartbeat beneath her ear.

'This is nice, I feel better already.' The regular thud, thud in her ear was hypnotic and her eyelids were drooping. 'It's like calm water after a storm.' There was so much more she wanted to say, but it was all lost in a jumble of murmur as she felt herself sliding into an easy sleep where the tangles in her mind were miraculously straightened out.

She needed Stephan because she loved him. It was why she had never needed any other man, she hadn't loved any other man. How could she when she still loved Stephan? A love she had denied—as if mere denial could kill it—just how ludicrous could you get?

Maybe he was flawed, but it made no difference. All that was left was honesty, admitting that he was the centre of her world, that life without him would be grey and empty; but with him her heart would be broken all over again. She wanted no more of that, but it was coming so she would have to grit her teeth and get on with it. And having made up her mind to take what little heaven was offered and leave the future to take care of itself, Manon slid deeper into a peaceful sleep.

When she woke for the second time, she was alone in the bed, and the autumn sun was a blaze of gold that lit up the dark corners of her mind and made her remember that she was supposed to have taken over the supplying of meals. She showered and dressed at top speed, and hurtled downstairs, only to find Battle performing miracles on the cooker and the kitchen full of the aroma of frying bacon.

'Daddy's still on the phone, he's been there for simply hours!' Fennie smiled at her over a mound of cornflakes. 'Do you feel better now, Manon? He said you'd been sick and were very tired so we weren't to disturb you. I hope you had a nice time, but I'm glad you're back.' At this point the sedate little mask slipped and the child showed through. 'I waited up for ages last night! It's been awfully lonely since Harry went back to school, there's been nobody to do things with. Battle's all right, but he cheats at Monopoly, he won't teach me how to play Pontoon and he doesn't like cats, so now I only have Mollie's puppies. He's given all my kittens away except the tortoiseshell one I'm saving for Harry.'

In the background, Battle accepted the assassination of his character with stolid, smiling indifference, but there were no pregnant pauses, not with Fennie around. 'Have some of my cornflakes,' she offered. 'I'm saving the tokens for a free gift, but it takes so long when there's only me eating them. After breakfast, would you like me to show you the rest of the house? You only saw the dining-room last time you came and I want to show you my bedroom. It's one of the attics, I chose it myself because it's got a lovely, slopy ceiling and you can see miles from the window.'

Manon accepted some cornflakes and then a platter of bacon and tomato while she listened. There was no need to talk. Fennie was more than capable of talking for two even while she was eating and she didn't require any answers.

'And you won't be going away again, will you, Manon? Not soon, anyway. You'll stay for a little while, won't you? Battle says I talk too much—you don't think so, do you?'

'Not a bit, it's only natural you should.' Manon poured herself a cup of coffee. 'We're practically strangers and we have to get properly acquainted if we're to be friends, but we can't be friends if we don't talk to each other—and no, I'm not going away, I'm a permanent fixture. I hope you don't mind.'

'No,' Fennie was ingenuously frank and blunt with it. 'I like you, Manon, and I'm glad Daddy

married you. And can we buy Harry some riding-
gear for when he comes next? I've picked out a nice
pony for him at the stables—a quiet one because he
said he's never ridden before. I go five times a week
because I only started this summer when we came
here to live and I'm way behind the other children.
They're trotting and galloping while I'm still doing
exercises in the saddle, but next week,' the small
face attained a seraphic expression, 'I'm going to
trot!'

'Spare us, Fennie!' Her father, finished with the
phone, had come back into the kitchen. 'Stop
talking now and finish your breakfast before you
run out of breath,' but it wasn't a scolding and
Fennie obeyed with a cheerful grin.

'I shall be in town all day, Manon.' As he said it,
Fennie groaned and Manon felt like doing the
same, but she kept her expression cool and pleasant
as he continued, 'I'll be home tonight, I'll try to
make it in time for dinner, but if I can't, I'll phone at
about five. Business, Fennie,' he added as his
daughter groaned again.

'More coffee before you go?' Manon picked up
the weighty pot and waved the spout in his
direction, but he shook his head while his dark eyes
flickered over her with a gleam in their depths she
didn't understand. Fennie had finished off the last
scrap of her bacon and was industriously mopping
up egg from her plate with the last of her fourth
bread roll. Stephan's eyes slid to her, then back to
Manon, but now they held a wry look before the
heavy lids fell and left his face expressionless.

'Stay with Manon until your tutor arrives,
Fennie.' It bordered on an order, but only just.
'Show her round, help her to get used to the place.

We don't want her to feel lonely.'

The little girl, her mouth full, nodded emphatically, and at last achieved speech. ''Bye, see you tonight, Daddy,' she said phlegmatically, removing her hungry gaze from the rack of toast and raising her hastily wiped mouth. Stephan avoided it—there was still some egg remaining at the corners—and gave her a swift hug. Manon abandoned her second cup of coffee and rose swiftly to follow him out.

'In all the TV ads, when a husband leaves to earn the daily bread, a loving wife goes with him as far as the door,' she managed smoothly to explain a purely reflex action. 'There's nothing meaningful about this, I'm just getting into the part. It's not the broad gestures but the little details that count in a really good performance.'

'But we have no audience,' he pointed out suavely, bringing a flush of chagrin to her normally pale cheeks.

'We have Fennie,' she reminded him softly, 'and children always notice little things.'

'So this gesture is for my daughter's benefit?' He sounded almost disappointed and the warm glint in his eyes made her feel petty and small-minded. He was holding out a hand to bridge the gap between them, she could feel herself weakening and almost took it before she recovered and snorted.

'It certainly isn't for yours!' But even as she said it, she could feel the smile growing on her face and the giggle—how could she be so juvenile?—in her throat was irrepressible. 'Off to work, laddie,' she placed both hands on his chest and pushed, but only gently. 'Extra effort from now on,' she reminded him. 'There's going to be an increase in your housekeeping bills!'

'A mere bagatelle.' Stephan waved it aside with a smile as he stepped through the door. 'I'm saving on a housekeeper's wages, and as a married man, I shall receive a larger tax-free allowance on my income.'

The tour of the house gave Manon a view of how the other half lived and it made her feel rather depressed. Luxury was one thing, but all this space cried out to be lived in. Fennie seemed to take it for granted that there should be so many beautiful rooms, but Manon wrinkled her nose at them. It would be nice to be able to put up visitors, but it was evident, even to her untutored eyes, that nobody had ever visited. The house looked as though it had been furnished by remote control and never used.

Each room had a different colour scheme, yet they all looked the same, like pictures cut from a *Good Housekeeping* manual. Colours matched and contrasted just as they should but with an air of impersonality as if this were a show-place to be looked at, not to be lived in. Only the kitchen, a small sitting-room and Fennie's attic bedroom were in the least homelike.

'You do like it?' Apparently, Fennie was sensitive to atmosphere, her dark eyes—so like her father's—were clouded with anxiety. 'You won't always be away? Daddy promised it would be a proper home like other children have and that maybe, later on, I'd have a little brother or a sister. When you were little, Manon, you had Harry, but I've never had anybody but Daddy since Grandad died.'

'Promise,' Manon said recklessly, and damned the consequences before the oddness of the remark hit her, but this wasn't the time to be asking questions and she soon forgot about it. Fennie's anxious little face twisted her heart. She remembered her own childhood so well; it had never been luxurious, but wherever her father had been sent, they had all gone together as a family, and her mother had made wherever they had lived into as near a home as was possible.

'A proper home, Fennie.' She squeezed the narrow little shoulders comfortingly and cast caution to the winds as she quoted from her dead mother's list. 'With all the trimmings. Birthday parties, Christmas parties, dunking for apples on Hallowe'en—you can have your friends to stay and Harry will be coming during the school holidays.'

Fennie seized her arm and started towing like a pit pony. 'Now come and see my bedroom, Manon, it's super, and there's another attic just like it. I think Harry would like that, don't you? It's empty, so we could have the decorators in straight away and we could go and buy some things for it so it's ready for him for half-term.'

'Furnishing a room's an expensive business.' Manon halted breathless at the top of a flight of stairs. 'Hadn't we better wait until we can talk it out with your father——?'

'If you think that's best, but we don't really need to.' Fennie's little face showed a mixture of disappointment and obstinacy. 'If you say it's all right, then it's all right, and I can pay for it all myself, you know. I've got millions of money in my piggy bank!'

'Which is where it had better stay.' Manon watched the small mouth droop and hugged the child encouragingly. 'We'll get together with your daddy,' she added, 'have a proper council of war to decide what's best to do. My father always said things went better and quicker if they were well planned in advance.' It gave her a strange sense of satisfaction to see Fennie smiling once more.

Fennie beamed. 'Mr Bennet, my tutor, will be here soon, he's a bit late, but I expect it's because of his baby. It's a new one and it cries a lot at night and he has to nurse it because his wife's not very well and needs her sleep. But when he comes, he can help me put Harry's room through the computer. He can telephone around to get all the prices and sizes of the things we'll need and I'll feed them in and get a print-out so we have some figures to show Daddy this evening. That's good planning ahead, isn't it, and it'll be better than an ordinary maths lesson.'

'You have a computer?' Manon widened her eyes and Fennie giggled.

'Of course! Mr Bennet says I'm an infant progidy or something. Oh, and I've just remembered, we can use the graphics thing to make all the furniture fit nicely. That's how I learn my geometry.'

Battle's voice, a parade-ground yell, came thundering up the stairs and Fennie paused with her hand on the door-knob. 'Mr Bennet's here!' She sounded delighted as if she couldn't wait to get down to work. She started down the stairs to halt in mid-progress and turn a wheedling face upwards.

'Make plenty for lunch, please, Manon. Mr Bennet has it with us and he's so very thin. I don't think he gets enough to eat.'

'What and when?' Manon almost moaned as Fennie went scampering down the flight to turn on the landing and give her a parting wave.

'Milk for me and tea for Mr Bennet with biscuits

at eleven. Bangers and mash at one, that's my favourite, and Mr Bennet eats anything,' she called back up the stairs. 'With apple pie and custard for afters!'

CHAPTER SEVEN

AFTER a quick look around Fennie's attic, Manon followed her down the stairs, sidling round the cleaning woman who was desultorily dabbing at the banisters with a duster. An infant prodigy, she shrugged, what else could be expected from a child of Stephan's? Not normality, that was for sure! But a normal little girl in most things, she reassured herself, grimacing at the thought of life with a juvenile egghead. It could have proved very wearing. And Fennie lit up for horses, which was a thoroughly normal trait and very good for her. At least she had plenty of healthy exercise and a chance to meet other children and compete.

Manon groaned silently at the mere thought of addiction to a computer. To one who had never been able to work a pocket calculator with any degree of success and who still relied on a pencil and the back of an envelope for anything more complex than thirteen multiplied by three, a computer smacked of an outsize intelligence which might take some getting used to. But setting aside—for the moment—the problems that might be caused by living with a youthful genius and concentrating on basics, she thought she could find plenty to do in the house to occupy her time, and on impulse she stopped by the daily woman and suggested a cup of tea and a chat in the kitchen in half an hour.

Battle had vanished into the annexe, leaving the kitchen looking as spotless as an operating theatre and about as welcoming, so Manon used some of the half-hour to cull a bunch of late roses from the garden, dump them in a pottery jug and stand them on the windowsill. It wasn't much, but the colourful petals and the green foliage helped by adding a humanising touch to all the spotless white and stainless steel.

The daily cleaner—she preferred to be called Violet—was depressed, too much was being demanded of her. With no housekeeper, there were extra duties that interfered with her routine, and her bunions wouldn't stand the pace. Manon, scared stiff of being left cleanerless, comforted her with fulsome praise for the spotless condition of the house, several cups of tea, digestive biscuits and an increase in pay of two pounds a day; clearing her conscience of extravagance by the thought that Stephan could very well afford it.

Battle, the soul of tact, confirmed—on his way through the kitchen with a bucket of logs for the sitting-room fire—that Miss Fennie's favourite meal was bangers and mash followed by apple-pie and custard, and that the 'tutor bloke' ate anything put before him.

'I thought she'd be on to you about that. It being your first day, so to speak.' A grin broke up his chunky features so that they looked more plastic and less like a surrealist wood-carving. 'She'd have it every day if you let her, but the boss says no more than once a week. Bangers in the fridge,' he added, 'apple-pie in the freezer, and I've cleaned the spuds for you.'

Fennie's choice was all right for lunch and blessedly easy to prepare, but Stephan would expect better for dinner, if or when he came. Manon's knowledge of cooking came mostly from having watched her mother, and memory came to her aid as she recalled things done with chickens or beef in a casserole when a meal was only on the 'possible' list and not a certainty. She searched every cupboard, drawer and shelf but failed to find a cookbook, so it would have to be by guess or by God.

The instant success of the simple lunch encouraged her and when the remnants of it were cleared away and she had made and drunk a leisurely cup of coffee she gave her mind to dinner. Drawing on memories, she jointed the chicken which she had put to thaw and set about dinner preparations as she had so often seen her mother do. Her only regret was that she had not paid more attention in those happier days, but regrets were a waste of time and Battle already had his orders. He was to buy her a simple cookbook at the earliest opportunity, like tomorrow morning!

Stephan was late and Fennie, already fed and ready for bed in slippers and a dressing-gown over her pyjamas, was lying in wait for him with a fistful of computer print-outs. She oozed practicality and confidence as, before Stephan had laid his briefcase aside in the small room he used as a study, she came straight to the point; hitching herself on to a chair on the interviewee side of the desk and waving him to the bigger chair in the more important position behind the blotter.

'It's Harry's room, Daddy. We've chosen the other attic for him and Mr Bennet told me about a local firm that makes fitted furniture out of real wood, so we rang them for prices. Here's what it's going to cost.'

Over the top of his daughter's head, Stephan raised his eyebrows at Manon, who shrugged helplessly and wagged her head as if to say, 'Don't blame me, I had nothing to do with it.'

'It's reasonable.' He ignored everything except the total on the last sheet. 'But Harry may not want . . .'

'But he does, he told me so!' Fennie's small jaw jutted in excellent imitation of her father. 'You told me everybody needs a place of their own to go to sometimes and this will be Harry's, but we'll have to start on it straight away. There isn't a lot of time, you know—it's only a few weeks until half-term and I want it to be ready for him when he arrives.'

'Then get started on it first thing in the morning.' Stephan was treating Fennie as if she were an adult, he wasn't talking down to her; neither was Fennie whining or wheedling in a childish fashion. These two understood, loved and respected each other, and Manon, standing outside the charmed circle they made, experienced a sudden chill. She had a vision of Stephan and Fennie, still in that closed circle, but with her own child sharing the togetherness. The three of them close and herself; still on the outside, wanting in but never admitted.

It was she, not Fennie, whom Stephan treated as

a child; a contrary, badly behaved, unreliable child; a grown-up child whose mistakes couldn't be excused by youth. That was the way he saw her, would always see her until the time when he didn't have to see her any more. And Harry was growing fast, in a few short years she wouldn't be so important to him and then she would have nobody. She shivered and abandoned her gloomy thoughts to hear Fennie and her father still talking, Fennie explaining things with a clear, decisive practicality and Stephan putting in a word here and there, not indulgent but understanding. Listening to them, Manon was beginning to believe the 'infant prodigy' thing, and Stephan's next words seemed to confirm it.

'. . . and although I know you could handle it, I wouldn't advise you rang the firm.' A real smile curved his lips and Manon felt a sharp stab of jealousy, because he never smiled at her that way. 'Remember what happened when you tried to buy the terrier by phone.'

'Grown-ups are so stupid sometimes.' For the first time, the little girl seemed just that, a little girl. A hot flush mantled her cheeks and she contorted her small face into an appalling grimace. 'They treat me as if I was a mere child, but I s'pose you're right. They'd ignore me and wait till you were here, then ring for confirmation like that woman at the kennels.' The grimace vanished, to be replaced by her usual, confident look. 'Then perhaps Manon had better start it off, and I did want to do it all myself.' She heaved a huge sigh. 'Manon, you know what to do? You phone and say "this is Mrs Vestris speaking". That'll make them sit up and take notice, then you tell them to send somebody round here straight away.'

Manon made her own grimace when Fennie, obedient, had gone off to bed clutching her precious print-outs and a mug of cocoa. Stephan had showered and changed from his city suiting into comfortable slacks and a suede-fronted cardigan over a cream silk shirt and Manon was setting her casseroled chicken on the table in the breakfast area of the kitchen. She had inspected the dining-room, a vast place full of well polished mahogany, and decided her cooking wasn't worthy of it.

'What's that?' A wave of Stephan's fingers indicated the dish.

Manon sounded doubtful. 'My mother called it Chicken Marengo, but I think it's just a casserole. I've never made it before. To be honest, I've never made anything much before except sausage and mash and the things we ate on the boat, so you're my first victim. I hope you survive! You did say you'd attend to the wine,' she reminded him.

'A first effort? Mmm, cause for a celebration.' He gave her a sidelong look and went off, to return a few minutes later with a misted bottle and two champagne flutes which he placed on the table while the bottle went straight into the fridge before he sat down, shook out his napkin and helped himself from the dish. Manon watched with bated breath as he raised a forkful to his mouth and only relaxed when he nodded approvingly.

It was infantile to feel so pleased at so small an achievement, but she couldn't help it, and a smile lingered round her mouth as she pushed her own serving round and round her plate because she was too full of relief to eat, and her eyes shone as she watched him steadily demolish what remained in the serving dish and then go on to make a hole in the chilled orange soufflé she had whipped up for dessert.

She drank thirstily of the champagne when it was poured, feeling the bubbles fizz on her palate until she was quite lightheaded, but she managed to follow him calmly when he carried the coffee-tray into the small sitting-room where Battle had lit a log fire against the damp mists that rose from the river. Stephan poured the coffee and paused with her filled cup in his hand.

'My compliments,' he said gravely. 'That was a very pleasant meal, but I noticed you didn't eat any of it. Did you by any chance include a hefty dose of poison?'

'I wasn't hungry.' She made a moue. 'And the name's Lucas, not Borgia.'

'The name's Vestris, not Lucas,' he corrected softly and as their fingers met under the coffee-cup she wanted to cry out, 'Please, hold me; kiss me as though I were a friend, not just a sex object.' But the words refused to stumble from her lips, they just agonised behind her eyes and she moved like an automaton, stirring and sugaring her coffee, waiting for him to break the silence.

He knew she was off balance, damn him, and he kept her waiting. She had expected him to get himself a drink, but he seemed as moderate about alcohol as he was about everything else. Personally, she would have liked to sink into an alcoholic haze so that she could allow herself to tolerate loveless lovemaking. The trouble was she couldn't tolerate the alcohol either.

'You've had a good day?' asked Stephan. 'You're finding your feet?'

Manon made a bundle of all her wishes for a happy ending and threw it on top of the fire, the right place for wishes which could never come true.

'Mmm,' she answered him quietly. 'I think I'll be able to cope. By the way, I've increased the cleaner's wages,' she added. 'I hope you don't mind, but her bunions were hurting and she now has extra work. The same hours but two pounds a day more, I thought that was fair.'

'And Fennie?' He raised an eyebrow. 'She's no problem?'

'N-no.' Manon's slight hesitation raised his other eyebrow and she hastened to explain. 'Not now I realise I'm coping with a superior intelligence. I shan't be tempted to tell her fairy tales or buy her a doll.'

'I believe she's very fond of fairy tales.'

'Mmm.' Manon gave a definite nod. 'But d'you know her idea of a fairy tale? It's Tolkien's *Lord of the Rings*! She quotes from it!'

'Inaccurately, I expect,' Stephan said encouragingly. 'And this phase mightn't last, I have it on good authority it could vanish with puberty.'

'Sorry, but I don't think I'll be here to see that.' Her voice became tinged with acid. 'I'd like to though just to see how you'd cope with an ordinary run-of-the mill teenager!'

'Same as I cope with you, Manon.' The dark eyes
held a gleam that could have been amusement. 'I
shall keep her busy!'

And that was true, Manon thought as she almost
crawled up the stairs to bed. She had the odd feeling
that her feet had hardly touched the ground since
her wedding-day. She had been kept busy or on the
move with a vengeance, and tomorrow would be no
different. Hardly time to think properly, and after a
sketchy shower, she scrambled herself thankfully
into bed.

But she was cross with herself. She should have
asked Stephan about his day, shown a little interest,
but she had been too intent on her own and Fennie's
doings. Her trouble was that she was self-orientated. She must have murmured it aloud. Stephan
padding in silently from the bathroom caught her
mumble.

'Who's self-orientated?'

'You are,' Manon defended herself wearily, and
was surprised when he slid into the bed beside her,
took her into his arms, placed a fleeting kiss
somewhere in the region of her forehead and told
her to go to sleep. She didn't need telling twice,
there was peace and security in his arms. She
pretended to herself there was also love and drifted
off to sleep, almost believing it.

Some time during the night, she woke, opening
her eyes to a world made colourless by moonlight, a
symphony in white and gun-metal grey, white
sheets and pillows and Stephan's face dark against
them and the weight of his arm across her breasts.
Moonlight and sleep robbed his face of life, turning

it into a beautiful, smooth mask. She lay very still, looking at it for a long time. There was something almost defenceless about the relaxed curve of his mouth and the closed eyes with their fringe of silky lashes.

She moved slightly and felt the arm tighten about her—even in sleep, he didn't let go completely— and with a little sigh, she snuggled closer, turning her face into the smooth skin of his shoulder, feeling the slightly damp saltiness of his skin against her lips. It was only a feather-light touch, but it roused him. The arm tightened even harder about her, the lashes quivered and his eyes were open while the moonlight lit the curve of his mouth.

'Mmm?' It was a question without words.

'Mmm.' It was an unnecessary answer and she gave herself up to the brief, transient glory because these moments were precious to her, and one day, the memory of them would be all she had left.

'Damn instructions, damn security and damn everything!' Manon muttered the words through clenched teeth as she peered down from the bedroom window at the workmanlike estate car sitting innocently on the gravel drive. Above her head there was a loud thump and she could almost see the ceiling shake while the pendant lamp in its centre swung about madly.

And damn Fennie and her project as well—she would be thankful when it was finished, although the fitted furniture firm had caused very little trouble until today. But today they were installing the shelving and cupboards which were to run round two walls of the attic, and Violet, bunions and all, was on duty in the kitchen, keeping up the constant supply of tea necessary to sustain the workmen.

Fennie, of course, was at the centre of operations, watching every process with an eagle eye, talking knowledgeably about dovetail joints and thoroughly enjoying herself, although she had been deprived of her morning lessons—Mr Bennet's new baby had croup and he was *hors de combat* after two sleepless nights—and Manon wished for freedom.

The key to that freedom was standing on the drive, had been standing there for the past half-hour, and if Battle, who had parked it there, had left the keys in the ignition, that freedom was within reach. She took a last look at her reflection—the black silk suit still looked good, although it fitted more snugly than the last time she had worn it—picked up her flat black bag and sped down the main staircase, her high-heeled, black patent pumps clicking swiftly with the speed of her going.

Breathless, she arrived on the drive and inspected the car, a little bubbFe of excited fear forming in her throat as the door clicked open under her hand and she saw the keys still in the ignition. Escape was possible, only for a few hours of course, not for ever, and she had already rung Polly to expect her but to understand if she couldn't make it, and she had added a mumbled excuse about transport.

With a firm finger, she depressed the locking system just in time. In the rear view mirror, she caught a glimpse of Battle, bucket and wash-leather in hand, emerging from the annexe which housed the garage and his own quarters. Her gay, uncomplicated smile was a travesty of the real thing, but it would have to do, and she rolled down the window a couple of inches to wave her fingers through the narrow aperture.

'Off to Town,' she shouted gaily. 'Back by five!'

Battle hesitated, and that hesitation bolstered her courage so that her stiff smile turned into a cheerful grin.

'More than my job's worth, Mrs Vestris.' He had come to a decision and he was going to put his foot down. 'Now come out of there, you know the boss's orders. You got to have somebody with you and you know I can't come. Miss Fennie's riding this afternoon. How am I to take her when both the cars is otherwise engaged?'

'The Land Rover?' offered Manon, her grin widening. 'The one you spend so much time cleaning!'

'But that's mine!' He sounded outraged when she laughed aloud.

'And you don't want to get it dirty? I'll help you clean it tomorrow. Oh, come on, Battle, don't be difficult. All I want is a run up to Town to see my friend Polly. I promise not to stop en route, not to pick up any hitch-hikers.' Manon heard her voice degenerating into a wheedle and pulled herself together, abandoning her grin for an expression of grim determination. 'Just you try and stop me! You'll need to put a bomb under the front wheels!'

By this time he had planted himself, bucket and all, in front of the car, almost as if he intended to push it back by brute force. Manon switched on the ignition, set her mouth in a straight line, went into reverse for a few yards, saw and understood his smile—he thought she was giving up—slammed the car into bottom with a tremendous screech of the gears, depressed the accelerator and drove round him, rocketing over a well tended flowerbed full of late-blooming dahlias, and sending a shower of gravel spraying across the lawn.

The gates were open, thank heaven, although it was a bit late to think about the consequences of trying to crash through wrought-iron, and she drove out triumphantly on to the road.

But she stepped out of the car on to the gritty London pavement outside Polly's place filled with an unreasoning and unreasonable guilt which had been building up in her ever since she had joined the motorway at Maidenhead.

She didn't want to get Battle into trouble, he had proved himself too good a friend in so many little ways and she was determined to be back in Henley long before Stephan arrived home. It would be a *fait accompli*, but she wouldn't make any secret of what she had done, so that if Stephan made a fuss, he would be able to see there was nobody to blame but her.

She and Polly fell on each other's necks, and after a cup of coffee and Polly's reluctant change from her indoor uniform of leotard and leg-warmers into something more suitable for street wear, they went out. They gave shopping a miss—Polly was short of cash until payday and she never allowed herself to touch what she called her 'Old Age Fund', the small amount she squirrelled away every month—and contented themselves with a walk through the Park, followed by a visit to the cafeteria patronised by aspiring but unemployed members of the entertainment world. It was a bit sleazy, but it had been Manon's refuge in the bad days. Everybody had always been sympathetic, and she had needed that to boost her busted morale.

That was how it had been, but today, there was a subtle difference in the atmosphere. It was as if she no longer fitted in, was no longer a part of the group, and it puzzled and saddened her. Polly put her finger on what was wrong when they arrived back at the cramped little flat for a final cup of tea before Manon started on the journey back to Henley.

'Don't be a dope, darling.' Polly was forthright as ever. 'You can't expect anything else. Maybe you still class yourself as a failure, but the others don't see it that way.'

'You mean they think I took the easy way out and despise me for it?' Manon was indignant, too hurt to be discreet. 'Don't they realise? I mean, the theatre was my life, but there was Harry. I had to think of him and his future.'

'No. I don't mean anything of the sort,' Polly denied vigorously, dropping into her contemplative position with a wry, 'I think better this way!' before she went on musing aloud. 'They don't despise you at all, there's not one of them who wouldn't have leapt at the chance you had if it were offered to them.'

'But they think I should still have gone back to the theatre?'

'You being you, I don't see how you could have,

angel,' Polly wrinkled her nose in concentration.
'Not and keep your self-respect. Everybody would
have thought and said your Stephan had pulled
strings to get you a part, they'd never have believed
you could do it on merit alone, and you know how
they feel about that sort of thing when it happens to
somebody else. When it happens to them, that's
different. But it was you who married a rich man.'

'And went up a rung on the ladder?' Manon
heard herself sounding bitter. She had counted
those others as friends; she had shared hopes as she
had shared sympathy, accessories and unladdered
stockings, but now the camaraderie was all gone.
Polly's crow of laughter pierced her gloom.

'Not gone up a rung.' She shook her head. 'Just
moved over to a different ladder! Face it, Manon,
you did the wise thing, so don't grizzle because the
Entente Cordiale with a load of failures isn't what it
used to be. You're not a bad actress, but in my
opinion, you're better out of it, you aren't ruthless
enough. Take a look at the successful ones; they're
hard, they're dedicated and nothing matters to them
except success. You could never be like that, it isn't
in you. You've got a heart and a tender conscience
where you ought to have nothing but driving
ambition!'

During the drive back to Henley and in between
rehearsing reasons and excuses for coming up to
Town without permission, Manon mulled over
what Polly had said; coming to the reluctant
conclusion that her friend had been at least seventy
per cent right. Had she been as dedicated as all that,
she would never have dallied about with Stephan

for a month in the first place.

Neither would she have let thoughts of her brother interfere with her career. Harry would have had to take his chance the same as thousands of other boys. If, when he was old enough, he had still been set on the Army as a career, he could have joined the ranks and worked his way up to a commission.

Ability was one thing, but ruthless determination was quite another. Stephan had that, but she didn't. And there was also the stray, sly rumour she had heard more than once—the whispers she wasn't supposed to hear—that Manon Lucas lacked the spark, that she got by mostly on her looks. She had always discounted them as jealousy, but could they be true? Perhaps she would never know now, because her next part, whenever it came, would be one which Stephan had pulled strings to get for her, so of course she wouldn't be able to take it!

A big car travelling behind her, matching the estate's speed mile for mile, pulled out and alongside her in the middle lane. She spared it a glance and went back to concentrating on the road ahead. Let it pass, she was quite content with her modest fifty m.p.h.—but the car didn't pass. It matched her speed exactly until the exit road when it suddenly accelerated, pulled in ahead of her and led the way off.

Manon read off the number plate, became aware of an unpleasant tightness in her chest and obediently followed while her mouth went dry, and she grasped the steering-wheel too tightly with fingers that had suddenly become almost useless.

This was what came of ploughing through Battle's precious dahlias. Anything else he would have forgiven—had she ploughed through him, for instance—but not the dahlias, they were sacrosanct. He had planted them himself and he tended them with big, blunt fingers more used to dishing out karate chops than fiddling with flowers. They were his pride and joy, she had ruined them, so he had put her on report!

It was quite a distance to the nearest layby, and Manon covered that distance with an exhibition of some of the worst driving in the world, to draw to a jerky stop within fractions of an inch of the immaculate bumper of the Rolls.

'So what!' she muttered aloud as she opened the door and swung her legs out of the car. 'He can't kill you, can he?' But she remained unconvinced. Perhaps, if he did, it would be better all round!

Stephan was also out of the car, approaching her swiftly, and they met where the bumpers just failed to meet. 'A bit of good driving, that.' She draped herself elegantly along the bonnet of the estate and contemplated the minute distance between chrome and chrome with spurious satisfaction. 'I doubt if anybody could have done better. Battle rang you, I presume to tell you I'd stolen a car, not to mention threatening to run over him if he tried to stop me, and you've been lurking . . .'

'Nobody rang,' Stephan told her blandly. 'I finished up in the office early, had lunch with a friend who's negotiating a couple of purchases for me, thought of the delightful surprise I'd give my loving wife by arriving home early and then spotted you on the motorway. You know the rules, Manon, I spelled them out for you. Neither you nor Fennie go anywhere alone!'

'That was the problem.' She pretended to give it grave consideration. 'Fennie and I had different ideas about what we should do with today and Battle can't be in two places at once. I thought Fennie was the more important. Oh hell!' as his face remained mildly enquiring. At least he wasn't looking as though he wanted to bite her head off, and that gave her the extra bit of courage she needed. 'I wanted to see Polly, I wanted to talk to somebody sympathetic and I was quite safe. You said you could look after yourself, so can I!'

'I didn't know you could drive.'

'There's a lot of things you don't know about me,' she interrupted, 'and of course I can drive—want to see my licence! Driving cars is a doddle, you should see me drive a tank!'

'A tank?' His eyebrows raised in patent disbelief. 'Oh no, Manon. That I can't believe.'

'Yes, I can; I did!' She lifted her chin and wrinkled her nose at him triumphantly. 'On a parade-ground in München Gladbach. I was only sixteen at the time,' she added honestly.

'Any casualties?' Suddenly his eyes were gleaming with an unholy joy, and her own lit with an answering smile.

'I missed the sentry,' she made it mock mournful, 'but I got the sentry box on the way back!'

'So today, failing a tank, you snitched a car and went off in search of tea and sympathy.' Stephen abandoned the temporary diversion and his black brows drew together. 'Did you pour out all your woes to Polly? If you need a father confessor, what's wrong with me?'

'How could I pour them out to you?' she laughed crazily. 'You're the cause of most of them! But please, credit me with a little discretion! I don't discuss either my marriage or my marital duties with anybody but my husband.'

'Duties?' She was convinced he was laughing at her. 'You perform some of them with a suspicious fervour. More like a labour of love!'

For a second, rich blood mantled her cheeks and then fled to leave her pale but undismayed. So what! It was a labour of love, and why should she be ashamed of it just because the love was all on her side? Suddenly she felt amazingly brave.

'Contractual obligations,' she corrected him pertly, 'and like any good employee, I have my employer's interests at heart. I perform over and above the line of mere duty!' And before he had time to reply, she went on briskly, 'Hadn't we better go home? Fennie will be getting ravenous, and I dare say you are as well.'

CHAPTER EIGHT

THE washing-machine clicked off and Violet's grunting cough—her usual means of drawing attention to herself—disturbed Manon as she began to transfer the load of sheets to the tumble-dryer. She gave a little sigh of aggravation as she pushed the last sheet into its yawning porthole, slammed the door and switched it on before she followed Violet out of the laundry room and back into the kitchen.

'A visitor for you, Mrs Vestris,' she said forbiddingly as if visitors shouldn't be allowed. 'I've showed her into the small sitting-room.'

Manon's mental processes started churning. A female visitor, a stranger to Violet, otherwise she would have been named. But the sort of female who was shown into the sitting-room? That ruled out collectors, flag-sellers and a host of other people whom the help kept standing under the porch out of sheer spite at having to leave whatever she was doing to answer the door.

Manon manufactured a sweet smile, looked at her watch, decided it was nearly time for the mid-morning break and suggested Violet should put the kettle on.

'Tea for me,' said Violet with a sigh of relief. 'Them stairs takes it out of you, specially the back ones what those workmen was trailing up and down to the attic. I'll make a pot of coffee as well, I dare say you'll be wanting it. I'll give you a call when it's ready.' Which meant the visitor was lah-de-dah, had treated her like dirt and she would die or give in her notice before she carried the tray into the sitting-room herself.

With a regretful glance at the pile of towels and pillowcases waiting to be put into the washer, Manon rinsed her hands at the sink, stripped off her apron and examined her face in the mirror to tuck back a heavy tress of hair which had come loose during her wrestle with the wet sheets.

'Yes, you do that.' Her hesitation was only momentary. 'While I try to get rid of whoever it is as quickly as possible. I'm too busy this morning.'

'Aa-ah.' Violet sounded doubtful, she muttered something under her breath and Manon left the kitchen with the impression that it was something like 'not get rid of that one so easy,' but it was only an impression, not a bit reliable, so she discounted it.

The larger mirror in the hallway showed her looking neat and trim in a grey flannel skirt topped with a cream and green striped silk shirt—hastily she rolled down the sleeves and buttoned the cuffs—and there was no make-up to repair. She looked good, not as though she had just come from coping with the washing. She even felt confident as she entered the room, but the confidence evaporated to be replaced with a chill curdle in her stomach, born of the memory of past humiliation.

There was no mistaking her visitor, she would have known that svelte figure, that immaculate blonde hairdo and the waft of distinctive perfume on a dark road at midnight when there was no moon, but just to be sure she waited while the visitor turned from examining a porcelain statuette of a simpering Georgian lady to give her a thorough once-over with cold blue eyes.

'Hello, Manon.' The first Mrs Vestris seated herself gracefully and waved to the opposite chair. 'Sit down, my dear—and please, call me Linda, otherwise we'll never know who's talking to who. I think we should get to know each other better, we've so much in common, don't you think?'

Manon had been upstaged before, but never so thoroughly—she felt like a housemaid being interviewed—and there was only one thing to do in that position, take the centre stage and be brutal about regaining the ascendancy. She didn't sit, she crossed the floor to stand on the hearthrug, looking down at her visitor. That was supposed to put one in control of the situation.

'Only Stephan, I believe,' she heard herself being hostile, 'but I don't understand the change in manner and vocabulary from the last conversation we held,' she observed flatly. 'Why have you come here?'

'To see my daughter, of course.' Linda tilted an exquisite profile, ignored the hostility and tried again when Manon remained silent. She turned her head and the profile dissolved into an equally exquisite full face which showed a lot of determination. 'Don't make an excuse that Stephan wouldn't allow it, he's already left for London. I wouldn't be here otherwise. As he's probably told you, we didn't part on the best of terms, but I want to see my child and this is the first time our dear Stephan has slipped up in his security measures. I took immediate advantage, of course. Ask her to join us.'

'Sorry, that's impossible. You've had a journey for nothing.' Manon's brain reeled under the implications crowding through it. So this was the reason for Stephan's security blanket—oddly, she didn't find herself blaming him, but he could have told her instead of letting her worry herself to death. Her excellent white teeth came together in an audible snap, there were things going on she didn't understand, and until she did, perhaps it would be better to play the dimwit.

Rather raggedly, she started again. 'Are you staying close by? If so, you could try again tomorrow, perhaps. Stephan took Fennie to London with him this morning, a visit to the dentist.'

At that moment, the telephone on a side table tinkled once and she jumped at the chance it gave her. Owing to some untraceable fault, every extension in the house sounded off when the kitchen phone was raised—Manon made use of it as a signal to Fennie and Mr Bennet that lunch was on the table, but now it meant that Violet had the coffee ready—and with a muttered 'Excuse me', she left her stance on the hearthrug and hurried into the kitchen.

Here, her initial suspicions were confirmed. Violet *had* been treated like dirt, and she wasn't over it. The tray was ready but the crockery was of the hard-wearing, kitchen sort—it all matched and nothing was chipped, but that was all that could be said for it—and there was no variety in the biscuits. Half a packet of Maries had been dumped carelessly on a plate and Battle had joined the help.

'Any trouble?' he asked innocently, but there was a pleasurable anticipation to light his eyes and Manon drooped an eyelid at him in a conspiratorial wink.

'Nothing I can't handle.' She gave him what she

hoped was a look of confidence. Battle had forgiven her for stealing the car and messing up his first attempts at gardening. In fact the little fracas seemed to have brought them closer together, but not too close; she had noticed he had never left any car keys about since. 'Give me a quarter of an hour,' she added, 'then come in and make like an immovable object.'

His answering wink was droll. 'I'll bring in the vacuum,' he offered, 'that socket's gone very awkward lately, might even need a new one. Wouldn't like anybody to get a shock.'

Her back-up team was doing her proud and Manon carried the tray back to the sitting-room with a grin which she immediately converted to a cool smile as she pushed her way through the door.

'Sorry to keep you waiting,' she apologised insincerely. 'I thought you might care for a coffee before you leave.' Putting the tray down on a side table, she poured coffee with hands that were surprisingly steady.

Linda abandoned her 'woman in command' attitude, she became all regret and not only at missing the opportunity to see her daughter. 'I can't apologise to you enough for the way I treated you the first time we met, but I hoped you'd understand.' Darkly mascaraed lashes swept down as tinted eyelids fell. Was that to hide tears or the lack of them? 'I knew he had a woman aboard, but I hadn't expected it to be somebody like you—so young, so obviously inexperienced. That was what made me angry. Stephan was always a lecher, I was used to it, used to the sort of women he had. I thought you'd be the same as the others, but you weren't.'

'Thanks,' said Manon drily. It was a feasible story; she would have believed it but for an inner caution and the fact that throughout the blue eyes had remained as hard as ever. Besides, so many things had been said that other time, things which she could neither forgive nor forget.

And then there were the hands! Linda's were pale, slender and expressive but not relaxed. Unconsciously, they grasped at things, grasped and held: her bag, her gloves, the arm of the chair, and they weren't saying what her mouth said. Any halfway decent actress could adopt an appealing expression, add a husky tremble to the voice—Manon herself was very good at that—but hands were always difficult. One had to be careful about them, control them because they could be a dead give-away. On reflection Linda's hands hadn't shown either sympathy or concern, only that confounded grasping.

'You were trying to save me from myself, perhaps, and you thought a string of four-letter words would make me see sense?' Manon added the question and waited for the reply, cursing herself for being suspicious when the reply seemed to come far too quickly, as though it had been rehearsed.

'Of course, my dear.' The elder woman's nod was perfunctory. 'I wanted to jerk you out of your fairy tale, make you see Stephan for what he was—a liar, a seducer, a man with the morals of a . . .'

'Yet you left your daughter in his care.'

'You don't understand, I had no option——' Linda broke off to turn a venomous glare on Battle as he clattered through the door with an outsized vacuum cleaner and dumped it in the middle of the floor.

'Sorry about this, missus.' A kitten couldn't have looked more innocent, and Manon snorted to herself and kept a straight face. Battle innocent? He was a past master at deception, even his English had slumped into a much more pronounced East London accent, and somehow he managed to look bumbling and awkward. She took a chance and played up to him like mad.

'Do you *have* to?' She made the enquiry in a helpless voice, beginning to enjoy herself—after all, this was what she did best, what she had been bought for—and playing the 'girl who had risen above her station and couldn't cope' routine for all she was worth.

'It's Violet,' Battle played back to her; he was the innocent suffering for the guilty and feeling injured about it. 'Had a nasty shock from this plug yesterday, so she said, and in here too. I thought I'd better check the socket while I was at it, the boss wouldn't like . . . and you know Violet, she's one to claim damages. Then we've got you and Miss Fennie to think of.'

'Oh dear!' Manon portrayed indecision, tugging at her hankie with nervous fingers—but unfortunately, it was a good strong one and refused to rip dramatically—while, out of the corner of her eye, she watched traces of emotion flit across Linda's face. Derision, irritation and lastly a tightly controlled anger; they were all there—except disappointment, and surely there *should* have been disappointment?—but it was the irritation that broke through.

'Isn't there somewhere a little more private?' Linda demanded shrilly, and for the fun of it, Manon ran through the unavailable accommodation.

'There's the kitchen, but I've got the dishwasher
and washing-machine going, the tumble-dryer as
well, and you can't hear yourself think! Violet's
polishing in the lounge and she hates to be
disturbed; there's Stephan's room, but he keeps it
locked when he's not in it and we can't talk here.'
She was ruefully apologetic, letting her glance stray
to Battle's unresponsive back in a meaningful
fashion. 'As you see . . . Some other time.'

Linda gathered up bag and gloves reluctantly,
cast a savage glance at Battle and whisked herself
out into the hallway. Manon followed and received
a look of contempt, but she kept her apologetic
smile going in between several humble 'I'm *so*
sorry's', and only relaxed when she closed the door
behind her unwelcome visitor and leant against it,
giggling hysterically but without any real
amusement.

The visit of Stephan's ex had something unreal
about it. Manon walked back into the sitting-room,
now vacated by Battle, and poured herself another
cup of coffee, drinking it black and sugarless in the
hope that it would stimulate her brain. Stephan's ex
had displayed several emotions; arrogance, wilful-
ness; and she hadn't bothered to hide her contempt,
but there hadn't been a shred of maternal love about
her. Except for the initial demand to see the child,
Linda had behaved as though her daughter didn't
exist, which was most unusual!

Back in the kitchen, Manon gave Battle a harried
glance. Several ideas and fancies were floating
through her head, but predominant was the mad
thought that she didn't want Stephan to know his

ex-wife had been anywhere near the house. Both life and Stephan had been a lot easier to cope with lately, as if she and he were making an effort to start afresh, so that this temporary arrangement would be as smooth as possible, but it was a delicate growth and she didn't want it spoiled in case it stopped growing.

Why should she think the mention of a visit from his ex-wife would spoil it? Manon didn't know the answer to that one, but she knew it would. Battle seemed to read her mind.

'People always say there shouldn't be any secrets between a man and his wife,' he observed enigmatically without raising his head from the bowl of potatoes he was peeling deftly, and his speech was much less slovenly.

'And you agree with that?'

'Big things, yes,' he looked at her over his shoulder. 'But sometimes . . . The way I see it, the boss has quite a lot on his plate just now. Big doings, lots of meetings, something important in the wind. No sense in bothering him about things we can handle ourselves.' The last potato was peeled and fell with a plop into the bowl, and Manon thought her sigh of relief would be audible all over the house.

'You think we can? Handle it, I mean?'

'Piece of cake!'

At one o'clock, Manon laid the table in the kitchen and checked the oven. Stephan had said they would be back for lunch and she wanted everything to be just so; a wild, silly desire she couldn't really account for. Since Fennie would have done all the suffering, she should have her favourite things to eat—you didn't have to chew creamed potatoes—and in case she couldn't manage the bangers, there was plenty of Stephan's Boeuf Bourguignon to share.

She didn't hear the car arrive, only Fennie's chatter and her feet running down the hallway, clattering on the polished tiles. 'We're back!' The little girl didn't look as if she had suffered a lot of pain. 'Do you want to see?' And she opened her mouth as wide as it would go so that the world might see where an obstinate milk tooth had been removed to make room for the second tooth growing up beside it.

'Not a tear.' Stephan followed his daughter into the kitchen, and Manon spared him a glance to meet the faintly quizzical gleam in his dark eyes. A little frown crinkled her forehead as she took a brief moment to study him. Linda had said he was a lecher, and she should know, but he didn't look all that lecherous! The curve of his lower lip was definitely sensual but, on the other hand, it was such a firm mouth.

She turned her attention to her pots and pans swiftly while her mind went on working overtime on what she knew of him, dismissing what she had been told until she had enough time to think about it properly. He had definite ideas, ideas which verged on the narrow-minded about some things. Look at the fuss he had made when he thought she had carelessly destroyed her baby's life! On the other hand, he went about his lovemaking tirelessly as if he were starving for it! That thought brought a hectic flush to her cheeks—well, she did as well, but only because she was addicted to him. She was no lecher!

Still flushed, Manon tipped the boiled potatoes

into the food-processor, added butter and pressed the switch, only to flinch when a long, cool finger touched her face and he murmured in her ear.

'Sickening for something, my dear, or just overheated?' It wasn't much, but it was more than enough. She kept her eyes on the plastic bowl and fought for control. It was a hard fight, but she conquered the remorseless ache in the pit of her stomach and managed to be tart.

'You try slaving over a hot stove, you'd get overheated!'

Fennie managed a sausage, spearing it whole on a fork and nibbling delicately at it in between garrulous bits of conversation. 'I shall go riding this afternoon, I feel quite well and I'd like you to come and watch, Manon.' And then she started up a chant. 'I've got a secret, I've got a secret!'

'I know!' Manon felt normality creeping back into her and gave the child a frightening grimace. 'You're going to do somersaults while cantering bareback! Thanks, but I prefer not to watch. Yes, I know I'm a spoilsport, but that's the way I'm made. I can't stand the sight of bruises and blood or broken limbs. Either yours or the horse's.' Fennie's disappointed burble was swiftly quashed.

'You'll go with Battle, as usual, Fennie.' Stephan was decisive. 'I need Manon with me this afternoon.'

Manon inspected her plate of beef with enormous concentration to pick out and set aside each little pickling onion. 'Matinee performance?' she muttered softly, hoping it would go over the top of Fennie's head.

'Only a quiet talk.' But his murmured answer was almost lost in his daughter's squeal of outrage.

'You promised, Daddy!' She abandoned her
sausage. 'You promised I could tell Manon!'

'And so you shall, as soon as you come back from
your riding lesson.' Stephan smiled another promise
and Fennie subsided. 'I'm only whetting Manon's
appetite,' he explained softly. 'Making her curious.
She doesn't know what we're talking about and
she'll be on pins all afternoon trying to guess.'

But Fennie was a generous child, she smiled
seraphically—doubtless thinking about a horse or a
computer program—and changed her mind. 'No,
don't do that,' she protested. 'I know what it's like
when I know there's a surprise, but I don't know
what it is. It's—it's frustrating,' she brought out
the—to her—new word with a pleased look at
having remembered it, 'and it makes me feel sick. I
hate it and I'm sure Manon does too. Shall we tell
her now, right this moment?'

'Up to you, Fennie,' shrugged Stephan, and his
daughter's sigh of relief wasn't just audible, it was
wholehearted and gusty as she launched into an
explanation.

'You see, Manon, there's this new play and
Daddy's taking you to see it when it starts. It's
what's called the premiére and it's going to be
awfully posh with photographers and everything, so
after I had my tooth out, Daddy said I could have
some money from my piggy bank to buy you a new
dress so you'd look better than anybody else. It's
lovely, all cream satin. And there's a coat sort of
thing,' she sketched it with her hands, 'green velvet
with a lining that matches the dress. You'll look
fabulous!'

Manon, conscious of Stephan's eyes watching her
every smallest reaction, twisted her face into an

expression of awed delight. 'It sounds gorgeous,' she murmured. 'I can hardly wait to see it—and there was me thinking you'd entered yourself for the Horse of the Year competition!'

'Silly,' Fennie was practical. 'I'm not big enough to ride a horse!'

'I won't go!' Manon gritted between her clenched teeth as she and Stephan stood in the porch watching Battle drive Fennie off to the stables, and when the car had turned out through the gates, she continued her wild protest. 'It's *Second Chance*, isn't it? I might have known you'd think up something diabolical for me. I won't go,' she reiterated, 'I won't wear your damn dress or the coat, this is just your way of rubbing my nose in it, isn't it? Taking me to the first night so I can watch somebody else playing the part I wanted, the part I needed so desperately. I never thought you'd be that cruel. Not just cruel, bloody sadistic!'

The arm which had rested lightly about her waist while they waved goodbye to Fennie became an iron band that forced her back into the house and along the hallway. Manon fought the power of that arm every inch of the way, kicking at his legs and trying to claw his face in her agony of despair. Not a lecher, a torturer; one who lulled away her suspicions, made her feel almost happy and then whoomph! Down came the axe, right where it would hurt most!

'Damn you,' she sobbed as he unlocked the door to his study and thrust her inside to slam the door behind them and lean back against it, barring her way, but Manon had ceased fighting, she wasn't big enough to take him on physically. Instead, she used her tongue.

'Damn you and damn you again! I wish I'd never set eyes on you, I wish I was dead. I tell you, I won't go!'

'Yes, you will, Manon.' Stephan was paying no attention to her hysterical outburst, he was treating her as though she were no older than Fennie and a lot less level-headed. 'We made a bargain and you can look on this as part of the deal. I backed this production, I shall be expected to put in an appearance, and you, my loving wife—who has more than a passing interest in the theatre—will be by my side and looking happy, very happy.' And when she flung herself in a chair and turned a set, white face to the window, trying to ignore him . . .

'And you'll wear what's been chosen for you.'

'I shan't *wear* anything,' she interrupted hotly. 'I shall be decorated like a bloody birthday cake! Why don't you spatter me all over with jewellery, insure me against fire, flood and theft and wave the policy under everybody's nose so they'll all know exactly how much you've spent on Cinderella! Or better still,' abruptly, her rage collapsed and there was nothing left of the fire but cold ash, 'why a dress even, have you thought about that angle? Then people would see exactly what you've bought. Not even a rag, just a compliant bone and hank of hair. Has it been worth it, Stephan? Don't you sometimes wish you'd put your money to better use?'

'What better use?' He raised an eyebrow. 'Any other woman would have cost a mint; she'd have demanded all the things you'd like to throw at my head.'

Manon couldn't even raise a smile, there was a bitter taste in her mouth and a dreadful ache in her chest; she thought it might be her heart breaking but it had broken before and she had got over it, she would get over it this time as well. The trouble was he had just reminded her of the impermanence of something she desperately wanted to be permanent; made her remember that the future was looming. A well-heeled future without any financial worries, but not the one she wanted. That one had Stephan in it.

She hadn't consciously tried to make it a workable marriage, but it was working, it *was*. And she didn't want to think of how little time might be left. Only a year, perhaps, and she couldn't afford to waste a moment of it. Desperately, she clutched at the rags of her self-control.

'What the hell am I making such a fuss about?' she demanded wryly. 'We both know I'll be there, but just in case you think it's because of anything *you've* said, let me put you straight. I'll go because Fennie's a darling child and I wouldn't hurt her by refusing to wear what she's bought for me; not for all the tea in China. I wouldn't hurt any child!'

Two long paces and Stephan had covered the space between them and his hands came so heavy on her shoulders, she almost staggered beneath the weight.

'I believe that now, Manon, I have done for a long time. Don't you remember? I told you when we were on the boat that you were secretive but honest. You hid your pregnancy, but you didn't terminate it,' he said simply, his dark eyes holding hers almost mesmerically, but if she expected anything more, a little apology, perhaps, she was disappointed—then she shrugged the disappointment aside. One step at a time with a man like Stephan, it would take a long while and a lot of loving.

'May I see the outfit?' she asked coolly.

'Within the week.' Stephan looked down at her as though he could read every thought going through her head. 'We bought it from the shop where you got your wedding-dress. You remember?' At her slight nod, he continued as though they hadn't been at each other's throats a few moment ago, 'A few alterations are necessary, but they still have your measurements.'

Manon felt herself filling with a dull acceptance. She would put on a show even if she had to watch Rachel Ashe playing the part she had coveted for herself; the part which would have solved all her problems. Why was Stephan doing this to her? And she didn't know the answer to that one either, but at least he wasn't still holding her lost baby against her, and that was a step in the right direction. With an effort she strove to conceal, she kept her voice steady, almost chatty.

'It will be nice to go out. The quiet, rural life can get very boring.' She shrugged, watching his expressionless face reflected in the window-pane. It wasn't true, she wasn't bored. She was desperately insecure, but he wasn't going to know that, not from her! 'I miss working,' she added. 'I miss the theatre.'

'I've just provided the cure for that,' he reminded her quietly, 'you'll be able to talk shop with the cast.'

'Thanks for nothing.' She was being ungracious, she knew, but she couldn't help it. 'I suppose I'll be expected to congratulate Rachel on a superb performance? You have no idea how I envy ...'

'Quite a few women might be envying you!'

All her hurt forgotten, she swung round in her

chair to face him. 'Envying me!' Her laugh was light and false. 'When they're all doing what they want to do, whereas I . . .'

'But they're not to know that, are they?' Stephan's hands weighed hard again on her shoulders. 'Leaving Rachel out of it, most other female members of the cast would probably change places with you like a shot, or aren't you actress enough to play your part convincingly?'

That jolted her pride. 'I shall play my part.' She ground it out flatly. 'I, or should I say we, will give our usual, impeccable performance. It's what I'm being paid for and I must be doing quite well, Fennie doesn't suspect, and children have inbuilt radar.' She embroidered on it. 'I shall play the sexpot and make bedroom eyes at you all the time I'm not fighting off the competition! This is the first time you've played angel, isn't it?' and at his nod, 'You'll be overwhelmed with attentions! After the first few minutes, I doubt you'll know I'm there.'

The tight grasp on her shoulder was released and there was a thread of laughter in his voice. 'I would always know exactly where you were, Manon, but don't be too convincing, and go easy on the bedroom eyes. Invitations like that can get you everything!'

'Freedom and a proper job?' she hazarded with a sidelong look to catch his reaction, and grimaced at his almost imperceptible shake of the head.

'You already have a job.'

'One more to my taste is what I mean.'

'But it is to your taste, Manon.' The old mocking smile was back on his face. 'Tell the truth, woman, it won't hurt anything but your pride. What you have is what you want, what you need. Me!'

'Bighead!' But her lips twitched into an involuntary smile. Somehow, the sharp, stinging atmosphere between them had dissipated, it had become warmer, calmer as if they were almost friends, and she felt almost lightheaded with relief. But she wouldn't let herself indulge in anything fantastic, like hope!

CHAPTER NINE

MANON and Stephan had driven up to London early
with the two big dress boxes resting on the back seat
of the Rolls, together with a small bag containing
her underwear, two pairs of silk stockings—in case
she laddered one—her shoes and make-up. They
had gone straight to the hotel suite where a light
meal was ready for them, and after a swift shower
and a slightly longer period than usual in front of
the mirror to do her face and hair, Manon had
wriggled herself into the dress.

It was deceptively simple with a very modest
neckline, but it skimmed her not-quite-so slenderness from shoulders to ankles as though she had
been poured into it. She was dubious about the
knee-high split in the narrow skirt, but without it
she would have had to shuffle along like a Japanese
geisha. The silk-lined evening coat, a big, swirling
thing of so dark a green, it looked almost black in
the folds, also suited her, and she did a pirouette in
her high-heeled green sandals to make it swing out.
Stephan came behind her and she thought she
detected a glint of admiration in his eyes, but one
could never tell with Stephan.

Turning away from the mirrors, she faced him
with a raised eyebrow. 'You like it? I had a dress
rehearsal at home this afternoon for Fennie's
benefit.' How easy it was to say 'at home' and how
little it meant. Referring to the Henley house as
home was a bad habit and one she would have to

teach herself to abandon before it became more than a habit, more like second nature.

'She thought I looked gorgeous—her exact words, so I'm glad I showed her,' she added defensively with a slight moue of self-derision.

'That was thoughtful of you.'

'Yes, wasn't it?' Manon creased her face into a smile and answered brightly, determined to appear normal, although she felt rather dead inside. 'But I had to do something to divert her. She was so disappointed that Harry couldn't come home at half-term after all the plans she'd made—you should have heard what she thought of the cadet corps and field exercises! But I've promised her autographs of as many of the cast as I can manage, she seems to think I've the entrée to every dressing-room.'

Manon's memory jigged momentarily on to her least-liked puzzle, one that had been festering at the back of her mind for the last two weeks. Linda hadn't called again; either in person or by telephone. Could it be that mother-love wasn't so pressing after all, or was there a deeper, murkier reason? She could never like the woman, and dislike was too temperate a word for the emotion that filled her every time she thought about Stephan's ex-wife. Hate was a better word. Plain unadulterated hate and distrust. Unconsciously, her lips thinned and her teeth ground together.

'You look as if you could bite a nail in half—are you still hungry? You haven't eaten much.' Stephan was almost accusing, so she covered up with a bright smile that didn't reach her eyes.

'I didn't want much,' she shrugged as she walked back into the boardroom-cum-dining-room of the hotel suite where the waiters had cleared away the remains of the meal. There was no trace that they had ever been there, and she wondered if that was to be the story of her life. Never to be remembered anywhere, not even the stage; just somebody passing through with nothing to mark her passing.

'Nervous?' Stephan followed her, like a big cat stalking a bird. Since they had left the house at Henley she had felt as though they were tied together with a short piece of string and her nerves, none too steady to start with, were becoming ragged with always finding him just behind her shoulder and watching her every expression.

'No, I'm not nervous,' she rounded on him sharply. 'Why should I be? I'm not taking the centre stage tonight.'

'Eaten up with envy, then?'

That brought a wry smile to her mouth and she gathered up her cream silk evening-bag with fingers that weren't quite steady. 'Possibly,' she shrugged. 'It would be no more than normal, given the circumstances.'

A chauffeur drove the Rolls from the hotel to the theatre and when they were decanted on to the pavement, Manon shivered. There was quite a large crowd—some minor Royal, a compulsive first-nighter, would be arriving later—and Manon blinked in the sudden brightness as a flashbulb exploded. Once in the foyer, she had an impulse to run backstage and wish the cast success, but Stephan's hand under her elbow steered her inexorably towards their box.

It was going to be a full house; the tiers of seats were filling rapidly and she was glad for the cast's sake. Stephan must have invested a lot of money in

this production but if it was a flop, all he would lose
was money, and he could well afford that. Her
thoughts were with the cast who had invested less
tangible things: hours of hard grind during rehear-
sals and all their hopes. Stephan might be able to
shrug off a failure, but to them, it was jobs and
confidence all resting on a fickle audience and a
load of hawk-eyed critics.

The house-lights dimmed, the rustling and the
soft hum of conversation ceased, the orchestra
started up and the curtains parted smoothly on
Rachel Ashe, alone and haphazardly packing a
suitcase between taking telephone calls. It was a
slow beginning but Rachel was handling it beautifully and it was a good audience, everybody was
paying attention.

Manon kept thinking she should be down there,
in front of the footlights, doing something, but after
a while the feeling wore off and she began to see the
play as a whole. Since she knew it all by heart, she
could identify the extra bits which had been
inserted in the script—they improved the scene,
gave it more movement, although actually there was
none—and Rachel certainly made it worth watching and listening to. Every little gesture, every
change in tone of her voice was a carefully studied
thing but seeming so natural, and Manon knew the
work that had gone into that seeming artlessness.

Rachel was also transforming most of Manon's
corroding envy into respect for a polished performance which she could never have hoped to equal.
The last shreds of it died with the roar of applause
greeting the final curtain call and the corpse didn't
even twitch. Manon knew *Second Chance* was going
to be a success, and she turned impulsively to

Stephen, her eyes glinting green and her normally pale face flushed delicately as she lifted one derisive eyebrow.

'You've got a winner on your hands—the only trouble is, what are you going to do for an encore? May we go backstage now? I'd like to see Rachel, she'll be needing a non-participant to boost her morale.'

'And you think you could do that?' Stephan held her evening-coat while she slipped her arms into it.

'Who better?' asked Manon with a slight smile. 'I *know* this is going to be a success, it can't fail, but Rachel won't feel that way. She'll only feel drained and doubtful, you always do until you read what the critics have written. Let's go now, Stephan.' She slid her hand through his arm and gave him a tug. 'I want to tell Rachel she was superb.'

In the leading lady's flower-bedecked dressing-room, Rachel Ashe was full of a glittering, synthetic brightness which was only skin-deep. Manon kept in the background, leaving Stephan to do the honours with a huge bottle of champagne and an even larger bouquet. She hardly expected Rachel to recognise her, they had only been together once, ages ago, and Manon, with only a very small part, saved from a 'walk-on' by a couple of lines of speech, had been little more than an extra.

So, when Rachel kissed Stephan and added the bottle and the bouquet to all the other bottles and bouquets which were being handed through the dressing-room door—the place was beginning to look like a cross between a flower shop and a liquor store—she was surprised by the leading lady's glad cry.

'Manon! Manon Lucas—but it's been years,

simply years! Darling, you look superb—but then you always did.'

Stephan murmured his congratulations and backed out, leaving them together, and as the door closed behind him, Rachel dropped her air of gay certainty—she could pick it up later when the necessity arose—to let the usual self-doubts show through, together with an exhaustion which Manon knew only too well, having experienced it herself.

'Don't let anyone in for a few minutes, Henry,' she called loudly to somebody in the passage outside, and then, pouring a couple of glasses of champagne from an already opened bottle, held one out to Manon while she drank thirstily from the other. 'We nearly met last year,' she added.

'Oh!' It was Manon's turn to be puzzled. What was so memorable about a 'nearly' meeting?

Rachel gestured largely with an eloquent hand, slopping champagne liberally. 'Manon, you *know* how it is. I'd been offered this part if the play ever made London, but I wasn't sure, and seeing's always better than reading. I wanted to see what you made of it, how you played it, because it wasn't going to be an easy part for me. One gets stuck with an image and it's generally fatal to change it. So I took the train up to Birmingham, bought myself a ticket and watched your every move. I would have come backstage after the performance, but there wasn't time, I had to get the train back for my kid's birthday party. Be honest and tell me I was wonderful! D'you think the damn thing's going to have a good run?'

'You were wonderful,' said Manon, and meant it. 'Not so intense, and it worked beautifully, but it always does for you. And the play will break records.' She made herself sound utterly confident. It wasn't difficult!

'Blast!' Rachel gulped at her drink again as though she were still dying of thirst; which she probably was, it was a wordy part. 'And I promised my kid a proper Christmas this year. Now I'll have to disappoint her again. That's the fourth time in a row. God, I wish I could change places with you, get out of the rat-race and have a reasonable home-life.'

'No, you don't.' Manon was understanding but brisk. 'Not really. You only think that now because you're worn out. Tomorrow, when you've read the critics, you'll be over the moon.'

'You really think so?'

'Certain of it.' Manon had stooped to place a gentle kiss on a cheek still tacky with cold cream. 'This play's got everything, pathos, humour—and most important, it's got you. You're all set for the success of the century and you wouldn't have it any other way.'

'And you'd like to scratch my eyes out because it's me and not you.'

'No, I wouldn't.' Manon had paused with her hand on the knob of the door, shocked by the realisation she was telling the truth. 'I won't deny there was a time when I would have, but not now. First, I'm not good enough, and second, I can't be that single-minded. Acting's an art and though I loved doing it, I've begun to realise I'm a housewife at heart. All I really want is my husband, a home and a few kids.'

'Enjoy yourself?' Stephan's voice came in the darkness of the car, and Manon rolled her head round on the headrest so that she could see his

profile. It told her nothing, not what he was
thinking nor what he was feeling. She had watched
him at the party after the show, he had seemed to
enjoy it, but with Stephan one could never tell, and
with a little sigh she closed her eyes. Would she ever
understand him? Would she even have time to try?
Meanwhile, there was a question to be answered.

'Oh yes! And learned a lesson,' she admitted
gravely. 'I felt like an apprentice watching a fully
fledged craftsman at work. You were quite right
when you said I wasn't good enough. I'm not and
never will be star material, that takes some quality I
don't have.'

'Single-mindedness?' he suggested.

''Spect so.' She stifled a yawn and kept her gaiety
going. There was nothing like planning ahead to
take one's mind off one's troubles. 'My mind's a
clutter, but I'm beginning to have the germ of an
idea. I think, when I've fulfilled my contract with
you, I might ask you for a bonus. Not a cottage, but
I believe I'd like to run a boarding-house, one that
doesn't smell of damp and boiled cabbage. I'm
getting a good grounding in the domestic arts and
my cooking's improving. By the time I've done my
duty, I should be quite capable of running that, or
even a small hotel, and then I'd always have a home
of sorts for Harry while he's still at school.'

'You could do what you call your duty and walk
away from your baby without a backward glance?'
Stephan was still staring straight ahead, closed up,
shuttered and unreadable.

'Oh no.' Manon shook her head firmly but kept
her voice light as if she were discussing all this
happening to somebody else. 'You'll have to get
Battle to throw me out when the time comes, but I'll

get over it. What I've done once, I can do again!'

'It hurt when you lost the child?' It was a quiet question, slid in so that it took her unawares. It was the first time he had ever asked her what she had felt about it, and it ruined her act. She couldn't stop the words forming in her mind, nor prevent them from spilling from her lips.

'Yes, it hurt! What do you think I am? Some unnatural creature without a spark of humanity?' she demanded hoarsely, then took a deep breath to burst into a torrent of words. 'For you, it was different. You only saw it from a distance. You had a report to read, I suppose—from your investigators. A few lines of print, easy to read, easy to accept. Something remote,' she threw in a quotation which seemed to be apt. '"In another land, and besides, the wench is dead!" But for "wench", read "child"! So you really don't understand anything at all!'

As far as Manon was concerned, that was the end of the conversation; she closed her eyes and pretended to sleep for the remainder of the short journey to Henley, but it was only a pretence. Behind her closed eyelids, the past and the future flickered like an old movie. But when everything was over would it matter to anybody but herself how much she hurt? Play and pay, but the payment went on and on, there seemed to be no end to it!

At The Willows, Battle swung the gates open for them, and when Manon stepped out of the car, she shivered in the cold night air. Damn Stephan, he had brought it all back, all the memories she had tried so hard to forget and all the future she didn't want to think about. She was cold all through, cold and silent without a spark of life in her, hanging

midway in space between a flimsy hope and an
almost certain despair. Stephan opened the door
and pushed her inside, into the warmth, but she still
shivered.

'You're overtired,' he said gently as he inspected
her colourless face and the defeated droop of her
shoulders. 'A hot drink, I think. Go upstairs, get
yourself into bed and I'll bring it up to you.'

Manon had sufficient control to stop the tears
that threatened to fill her eyes, but when she had
done that, all her energies were used up. She
couldn't even be bothered to take a warm bath
which might have heated her chilled body and she
was careless about her clothes. Her lovely dress was
tossed on to a chair although she summoned
sufficient energy to stuff her underwear in the
laundry basket. After that, she scrubbed her face
free of make-up, cleaned her teeth and slid between
the sheets.

Stephan came upstairs a few minutes later and
handed her a mug full of hot milk. She sniffed at it
suspiciously and wrinkled her nose at the fumes of
rum, but she sat up in bed sipping at it, while
gradually her shivering ceased.

'I've looked in on Fennie.' He came back from
the bathroom, smelling very nicely of something
masculine and with his hair damp from the shower
so that it curled slightly. 'She's dead to the world,
and although she wanted to be wakened the
moment we returned, I thought not. There's
nothing that can't wait until morning.'

Her milk finished and the mug set on the bedside
table, Manon had turned on her side and closed her
eyes, but she felt the movement as he slid into the
bed, saw the darkness beyond her closed lids as he

switched off the light and felt the warmth of his body against her.

'You looked very beautiful,' he murmured.

'My one and only talent,' she muttered without opening her eyes, and his snort of laughter dismayed her. 'You've no idea how much suffering it's caused,' she complained raggedly. 'If I'd had a face like the back of a bus, I wouldn't be where I am now!'

'Quite wrong.' He pulled her closer and she felt the touch of his fingers and mouth as he pushed her nightgown from her shoulder. 'You're a very talented lady, in fact. Shall we try the one you're best at?'

On the first Tuesday in December, Stephan was called away from the breakfast table by a telephone call. Half an hour later he left as usual, and Fennie started on all the questions she hadn't asked her father.

'I wonder who called? I hope it wasn't Mr Preston, because if it was,' her small face clouded, 'Daddy'll be late home tonight and I wanted to ask him about my plans for the old basement kitchen we don't use. Battle says he'll clean it up for me and there's room down there for a table-tennis table, a TV and video, a hi-fi and some chairs and things, and we can put Molly and the pups down there as well. Battle's always saying they're getting under his feet. Don't you think that's a good idea, Manon?'

Manon, swinging between delight and despair because she still wasn't pregnant, did no more than mutter an agreement as the little girl went on describing her plans, which were vast and comprehensive, even down to the colour of the rugs to be scattered about the stone floor, the pictures on the walls and the use which could be made of the old-fashioned ovens for such delicacies as roasted chestnuts and potatoes in their jackets.

During her monologue, Fennie made inroads on the toast until there was only one slice left, which she generously offered to Manon, who politely rejected it on the grounds that Fennie's need was greater than her own. Luckily Mr Bennet arrived early for once, and peace descended on the kitchen as the two master-minds departed computerwards with a new disc-program which was guaranteed to take the knots out of quadratic equations.

At eleven, Manon provided more sustenance for the workers, including Violet, and listened to the latest saga of the bunions with an expression of deep sympathy, and at one it was feeding-time again. She had made a hotpot, a very large one, but there would be no left-overs, there never were except for the small portion set aside for Molly, who preferred human food. Mr Bennet might look like a harassed, ill-nourished bag of bones, but he had the appetite of a ravening wolf, and Fennie ran him a close second.

At two o'clock, Fennie departed with Battle in the estate car for her riding-lesson—gloomy because it had started to rain and the lesson might be cancelled—and when they were gone, Manon covered her shirt and skirt with a furry-lined Burberry, hid her hair beneath a green paisley-patterned silk scarf, pushed her feet into flat brogues and went for a strictly forbidden walk by herself. She needed fresh air and solitude.

The rain was harder now, fat drops spattered her as she walked briskly along the road and a passing car made her think about Fennie and Battle. Nobody would be riding in this downpour, the lesson could have been cancelled and the children sent home; any moment she could expect to see the estate car, it would stop and she would be hauled back to the house, and she didn't want that.

It took only a moment to skip across the grass verge and into the strip of woodland which ran between the road and the river, to make her way beneath naked boughs and scuff through the carpet of wet, fallen leaves. This was another way to the stables and maybe the lesson hadn't been cancelled, just changed. Maybe the children were being given a tack lesson instead of the usual ride. Manon was covering her bets.

This other way came out at the entrance to a small paddock where the far gate opened into the stable yard, and she was just picking her way round a pile of horse manure when she nearly fell over Battle, who was sprawled face down on the muddy ground, a shovel and a small bucket by his side. She was opening her mouth to make a tart remark about the hazards of stealing manure when a whole load could be ordered and paid for when she noticed the blood seeping from a wound on the back of his head and she shut it quickly.

For a moment, she gazed at him disbelievingly; stooped over him to touch his head and roll it gently before she stiffened. This wasn't an accident, he had been hit, and hit hard enough to raise a huge lump and break the skin. Automatically, her thoughts flew to Fennie. Where was the child? The unspoken question sent her scurrying through the gate and into the stable-yard, where she found the horses all present and correct in their stalls but no trace of their riders and—her eyes widened in mystification—the estate car wasn't parked in its usual place on the side of the road.

Hastily, she scurried back to Battle, pausing only to dip her hankie in a rainwater butt and drag the scarf from her hair as she ran. Battle was still unconscious and he remained so until she bound up the wound on his head and—with a great deal of trouble—turned him over on to his back, when he opened his eyes to peer at her groggily.

'Lie still,' commanded Manon as she felt him tense. 'Don't try to get up yet. Just tell me what happened. Did you slip?'

Battle's first words were unprintable, so she waited patiently until he reverted to standard English. 'Slip? No, I didn't slip. Somebody hit me!' He sounded outraged. 'I was just getting a bit of the usual . . . Where's Miss Fennie?'

'I don't know.' She tried to keep her voice calm, but it wobbled alarmingly. 'I walked here through the wood. But the car's gone as well—at least, it's not where you usually park it. Until I found you here, I thought you'd already taken her home.'

Battle became wary, he didn't need to have things driven in with a sledgehammer, and she could almost see the wheels of his mind starting to turn.

'Chances are, if she couldn't find me and the car's gone, as you say, she's walked home.'

'The car *has* gone, but the chances are Fennie's gone with it,' snapped Manon. 'Remember our visitor?' Ever since she had found him, she had been avoiding that thought, but it had been growing steadily into a conviction. 'The one we decided wasn't worth bothering the boss about?' she added.

'Go on, rub it in.' He struggled to his feet, cursing

under his breath and grey of face. 'But no, it couldn't be that way. I left the hatch open, but,' he patted a jingling pocket, 'the ignition keys are here. Got to think what's best to do.'

'Telephone,' she offered. 'There's one in the stable office, I phoned here once.'

'That'll do,' he approved, swaying a bit and clutching at her shoulder to steady himself. 'Let's go to it, then.'

Manon started off, walking slowly, but when she felt the pressure on her shoulder slacken, she turned her walk into a run so that she was first at the stable office and in despair over the substantial padlock which held the door fast, but Battle was at her side almost immediately and grinning weakly at her expression.

'No bother,' he muttered. 'When it comes to security, people always economise in the wrong place. That wouldn't keep a kid out!' He raised a heavily booted foot and slammed it against the door. 'Must be getting weak,' he muttered as the door stood firm. His second kick made him an even greyer shade of pale, but it succeeded. The hasp was torn, screws and all from the doorpost, the padlock dangled impotently and he stood back to let Manon go in. 'Could have kicked it in wearing me slippers,' he bragged breathlessly. 'The boss'll be home by now, so who's going to phone, you or me?'

'You.' Manon made up her mind instantly. 'And then you wait here. I'm going back down the road. Maybe I'll find the car, or Fennie, or both.'

'Good thinking,' he approved again. 'It can't be far. Whoever took it could get inside to take the brake off, but they couldn't start it, they'd have had to push it. Here, you'd better have the keys.'

'Thanks,' she caught the bundle of keys he tossed to her. 'And while I'm gone, pray!' she muttered. 'I don't like what I'm thinking!'

It was one thing to have a suspicion, another to put it into words, and Manon was haunted by Linda's hard blue eyes and slender white hands which grasped and held tightly. She could almost see them grasping Fennie ... Driving the picture from her mind, she concentrated. The estate was dark blue, the light was fading, it would soon be difficult to see.

But it wasn't so difficult after all, although when she found it, the car was useless. It had been pushed down the road only a short way; over the verge—the tracks it had made in the softer surface were quite plain—through the screen of undergrowth and been allowed to run down a steepish slope between the trees where it had been stopped by the substantial trunk of a beech and Manon half ran, half skidded down the slope to give it a closer inspection.

The whole front end was caved in, the bonnet had sprung open, and she bent over the wreckage with a sense of doom, wondering if Fennie had seen it. Missing both Battle and the car, the little girl would have gone looking for them. She could have followed the same search as Manon, only been quicker about it, and after that, she could have run for home. It was even possible she and Fennie had passed each other in the wood, too far apart and hidden by trees to be aware of each other. That was looking on the bright side; Manon didn't dare look on the other.

She was turning away, not really seeing anything while she tried to work out what else Fennie might have done, when a sudden thrust between her shoulder blades pushed her off balance. She watched as the ground rushed up to meet her, felt her temple connect with something hard and was stupidly pleased it was her forehead and not her nose. She wasn't unconscious, she was only stunned, and though she couldn't think she could hear patchily. The sound of voices came and went like waves breaking on a shore. There were feet moving about her and voices; a man's tenor was saying something, and she strained to make sense of the words.

'. . . need to have hit . . . hard as that . . .' it protested, only to be interrupted by Linda's voice, a bit shrill and breathy with a vindictive enjoyment.

'. . . been asking for it . . . bloody little tramp, getting in my way . . . haven't you found the kid yet?'

'She's not on the road anywhere.' Manon's head had stopped ringing and she was hearing every word. 'We haven't a hope. It's getting too dark to see properly. We'll have to call it a day. Come on, darling, let's get back to Town before . . .'

'. . . and try tomorrow?' Through the fuzz growing in her head, Manon heard Linda, icy and disdainful. 'You're a fool! Stephan will have everything sewn up so tight we'll never be able to get near her again, and she means money, you bloody idiot!' Her voice rose in shrill exasperation. 'Money that should have been mine, and I want it. Why should I have to manage on a piddling little allowance when my daughter's sitting on millions!'

Manon lay with her eyes shut, listening, and a sweet content was all about her. Her head felt quite numb, it wasn't even hurting; she made a sound, muffled in the leaves that were clogging her mouth.

It sounded very much like a giggle, and then she felt the kicks, two of them, hard and vicious. One connected with her ribs, the second jabbed excruciatingly into the big muscle in her thigh and a thick blanket of blackness descended on her to blot out everything.

CHAPTER TEN

THE blanket of unconsciousness lifted a little to let sound and feeling through and Manon heard the snarl of a car taking off in a hurry. The row hurt her ears and she winced. A souped-up job, all noise and discomfort—her thoughts ran on indiscriminately—comfort was really a London taxi with room to stretch your legs. She tried to retreat into unconsciousness and moaned a protest when she was dragged back into the cruel world again by hands feeling all over her.

Foggily, she was aware of Stephan bending over her; she knew the clean, astringent smell of him, quite different from Battle who always smelled of carbolic, and she remembered the important thing.

'Fennie,' she muttered, and began to cry weakly; angry with herself for being so stupid. 'I can't find Fennie!'

'Safe at home.' It was the most comforting thing she had ever heard, but oddly the comfort didn't last; it swiftly turned into irritation.

'You took your time!' she complained unreasonably. 'Why can't you be where you're bloody well needed?' and as a muzzy afterthought, 'Your Linda's a bitch!'

'Not *my* Linda.' That came through clearly, and with a weak smile of content, she closed her eyes and drifted away into a black, velvety place where there wasn't any pain. She scolded irritably when she was dragged out of it by a bright light which hurt her eyes and a pungent clinical smell that tickled her nose. Then there were other hands feeling all over her and a strange voice which asked questions and wouldn't stop till she answered them.

"Course it hurts,' she grumbled. 'Lemme alone,' and batted ineffectually at the probing hands, squeaking indignantly when she was forced to swallow a bitter draught and, after a few moments, she went back into a blissful haze and ceased to function.

'Feel better now?' Manon heard the question, it dragged her back into life and made her cross. She opened her eyes to glare at the sympathetic faces surrounding her, crunching her fingers on the sheet as she wondered how much of what had happened was true. It had all taken on an eerie nebulosity as if she might have dreamed it.

She was in bed at home, and a certain freedom about her body told her she had been undressed and put into a nightie. Stephan, unfamiliar in his shirt-sleeves, wasn't taking his eyes from her; Fennie was bright with interest while, in the background, Battle had Harry by his side. Harry?

Her glare gained in intensity as feeling crept back into her body, a feeling she didn't like. She had been very happy, painlessly floating, shrouded in velvet in a black void, but now she was back to hurting. Ignoring the others, she concentrated on her young brother, and there was no welcome in her voice.

'What are you doing here?' she scolded. 'You should be at school.'

'Measles.' Harry sounded more joyful than sympathetic. 'Four in the sickbay and the rest of us sent home. Don't nag, Manon, I've had 'em, you know that, so nobody can catch them from me! I rang this morning and Stephan fetched me, we thought it would be a nice surprise . . .'

'. . . and it is, isn't it? A super surprise,' Fennie broke in artlessly. 'Harry's going to be here until January and it doesn't matter, 'cos I've had measles. It'll be the best Christmas ever! Oh, Manon, I'm awfully sorry you've been hurt, but Daddy says it's only a titchy bit, and you won't let it spoil Christmas, will you?'

'That's thanks for you!' Manon made a disgusted sound as Stephan, having shooed the others from the room, closed the door and stood looking at her. With another disgusted sound, mixed up with a groan, she dragged herself out of bed—waving him away imperiously—and stumbled across to where the electric fire was casting a warm glow on an armchair. She didn't quite make the armchair, her knees gave out just as she was reaching out to hold on to it, but she managed to collapse, more or less gracefully, on to the thick sheepskin rug and felt the chair at her back supporting her.

'I suffer,' she continued plaintively, 'but is anybody grateful? No, they're not!'

'I am.' Stephen picked her up and sat down on the chair with her on his knee. 'Just some bruises and surface scratches.' He sounded assuring. 'Nothing deep enough to leave a scar.' But the assurance didn't work. She had had a horrible afternoon, full of worry and fear. It had all turned out all right, but she was feeling ill-used!

Battle's head poked back around the door, making noises about 'a nice cup of tea', and she summoned up a smile, albeit a very small one. 'Panic over?' she asked in a throwaway voice, but it came out with a definite wobble.

'Over!' It was Stephan who answered her question, being very definite about it. He flicked a finger and Battle's head withdrew from her field of vision. She heard the bedroom door close again, and through it, Fennie's burst of high, excited chatter.

'You really like it, Harry! That's ace! Race you to the kitchen . . .' and came the thunder of their feet as they clattered down the staircase. Manon put a hand up to her head and groaned. Couldn't they do anything quietly?

'Noisy little brats.' Stephan's eyes were gleaming with amusement. 'D'you want them confined to the basement until you feel less fraught?'

'No!' Manon shook her head, but not violently, she was still convinced it would fall off if she wasn't careful. 'I shall never feel better,' she added with a shiver. 'How can I? If it weren't for me, none of this would have happened. Damn you, Stephan,' she raged impotently. 'Don't you dare be understanding! I'm wallowing in guilt and I *want* to wallow!' She wanted to go on, explain about Linda's visit, apologise for not having told him about it, but she didn't see how she could do that without involving Battle.

'Guilt?' He made no fuss about rising, lifting her with him and carrying her across to the bed. For a moment, she thought he was going to slam her back into it, but he merely dragged off the duvet to bundle it around both of them and carry her back to the chair, where he sat down with a thump that jarred her aching head. 'And you such a pillar of righteousness,' he continued as though there had been no break. 'Too narrow-minded for words! You won't even share the shower ...'

'Not righteous enough!' she denied violently, deciding to spread the blame around a bit. 'We ...' but the blame couldn't be shared. Men didn't think the same way as women. 'I, me, all by myself, broke up a marriage because I was to careless to think things out properly.' She knew she was rambling, but still the words kept coming.

'I should have known a desirable property like you would have a sitting tenant, but I didn't stop to think.' A hectic flush of shame coloured her pale cheeks, but she went on grimly. 'I met you in the afternoon and by night-time, I was in your bed, and we didn't even know each other! And you—weren't honest with me.'

The door was pushed open and Battle marched in with a tea-tray, so she tailed off into incoherency and gave him the ghost of a smile.

'How's the head?' she asked, hoping he would stay for a few minutes. Something was looming and she wanted to put it off as long as possible.

'Good as new.' Battle would have said a lot more, but Stephan gave him a basilisk stare, so he dragged across a small table to within arm's reach, put the tray down on it with a thump and departed.

A spoon clinked against china and Stephan held a cup to Manon's lips. 'Drink your tea like a good girl and stop talking nonsense.'

'I'm not talking nonsense,' she mourned as she took a cautious sip. It didn't hurt, so she took another. 'If, three years ago, I'd been a good girl none of this would have happened. There might have been no divorce and you might still have your wife, although I can't say much for your taste. What's so funny about that?' she demanded crossly as she watched his lips curve into a closed smile. 'What the hell are you laughing about?'

'You, darling!' The 'darling' got through to her so that, for a brief, delirious second, she almost made herself believe it. Stephan never threw endearments about and it could mean something. But perhaps it was just gratitude for creating a diversion.

'Listen to me,' he continued as he fed her more tea and she gulped at it avidly, watching his face with huge eyes, sad in her pale face. *'You did not break up any marriage!* Will you listen while I explain?' And at her nod, he continued.

'There was a time when I didn't believe in love, Manon; I was thirty years old and it had never happened to me. I thought I was incapable of it. There were women, of course—like any other man, I have needs—but I didn't love any of them, and I regret to say I didn't love Linda either. Her father and mine were partners and when mine died, I took his place on the board, so Linda and I were thrown together. I don't think she loved me either, but she wanted marriage—I believe it was the fashionable thing to do at that time, all the best people were doing it—so we married. Fennie was born, and after that, it became a marriage only in name. Linda had no interest in either me or the child. I could understand the former but not the latter, and as soon as the necessary time had elapsed—longer then than it is now—she petitioned for divorce, and since she had no feeling for Fennie, she didn't oppose my application for custody.

'The divorce took a long time to get off the ground,' he went on grimly, 'while Linda haggled for the best terms she could get, but finally it went through with the minimum of publicity—that might have been bad for the firm since any kind of split in the board of directors can cause a lack of confidence—and things were peaceful until Linda's father died. That was when the trouble started. He'd changed his will and Linda was no longer the sole beneficiary.'

'He left all his money to you,' Manon interrupted acidly, and was surprised at the shake of Stephan's head.

'Not to me, darling.' Again the 'darling' surprised her. 'To Fennie. There was money for Linda, of course, the income from a trust he'd set up for her, but it was only a fraction of what she'd been expecting and she couldn't touch the capital. Even with what the courts had stipulated I pay her, her life-style was going to suffer so she tried to get Fennie back. Legally, through the courts at first, but when she was refused, by any other means she could think of. She set up situations trying to prove I wasn't fit to have custody, and when those failed, she tried to get hold of Fennie, knowing I'd pay anything to get her back.'

'The half of your kingdom, perhaps?' Manon

sniffed disparagingly, but Stephan shook his head ruefully.

'Linda wants more than that, sweetheart. My income isn't big enough. She has expensive tastes, and Fennie's five million would go a long way towards paying for them.'

'Five *million*!' Manon went rigid with shock. 'Oh lord,' she groaned. 'And I thought Fennie was . . .' She looked horrified. 'Once she mentioned the "millions of money" in her piggy bank, but I didn't take her seriously.'

'You couldn't be expected to.' Gently, with one finger, Stephan stroked the curve of her mouth. 'May I continue?' Manon scowled and shrugged.

'If necessary,' she sniffed unforgivingly. 'How much more?'

'The worst and most important part,' he said wryly. 'Just over three years ago, I left Fennie safe with friends and came down to Chichester for a holiday, and I met a girl.' He paused significantly, pushing up her chin so that she was forced to look at him. 'She wasn't my usual type; not slick, sophisticated, and with the rules of the game at her fingertips. She was beautiful, sweet, generous and young, so young, and I loved her on sight. We had a wonderful month and then I had to go back to London, but it gave me an opportunity to arrange things. I came back to the boat with a marriage licence in my pocket, only to find you'd gone, without even a goodbye, and then, I think, I went a little mad.'

'Oh, Stephan!' Manon choked on tears while at the same time she filled up with a ridiculous anger at everything. 'Your fault,' she accused, rubbing away the moisture from her eyes with the back of her hand. 'How was I to know?' she demanded angrily. 'Do you expect me to have second sight so I know when a complete stranger's lying to me? Linda said she was your wife, she never mentioned a divorce, and she wasn't mealy-mouthed. She made it all sound . . . sound animal! And I *did* leave you a note.'

'Which I never received,' he answered flatly, and his arms tightened about her, painfully tight considering her battered body, but Manon didn't feel the pain, only the close enfolding arms, as if she never wanted to be free again. 'Typically Linda—getting you to write it and then whipping it away so that I'd think you'd walked out on me. How do you think I felt when I found you gone? I didn't know Linda had been to see you! What do you think I thought?'

'What did you think?' She cursed herself for asking, she didn't think she would like the answer.

'I don't believe I was capable of thought.' He touched her face with a gentle finger, wiping away a tear which had spilled over and run down her cheek. 'I was blind with rage and disappointment, half mad with loss. You see, once, when we were talking, the subject of divorce had cropped up and you'd wrinkled your nose and made a face as if you found it distasteful—some people do—but I was mad for you, I couldn't bear the thought of losing you. I wanted to get my ring on your finger and your signature on our marriage certificate before I sullied your ears with the sordid details of my first marriage.' He paused for a second and then continued with a grim desperation in his voice. 'You've no idea what your disappearance did to me, Manon. I stopped thinking, I could only feel and what I was feeling was a strange, perverted rage. I supposed you'd somehow heard about the divorce and I determined I'd make you swallow it, even if it stuck in your throat and choked you. I'd do it, if it took years! Love denied an outlet gets twisted, it wants to hurt.'

'It wasn't that!' she muttered raggedly and with an odd pride. 'I *had* to go before you came back. I knew if I saw you and you asked me to stay, I'd stay even though I'd feel guilty.'

'You didn't act guilty—in Chichester,' he pointed out gently. 'Not with me. You didn't even blush!'

'That's right,' she scolded, 'blame me! "The woman tempted me", it's been the man's excuse way back to Adam! Equality doesn't mean a thing, even now when we're supposed to be equal. Go on,' she urged, seeing a slight smile curve his lips, 'have a good laugh while you're about it! I loved you then, I love you still! I'm a damn doormat! And I don't care about divorce either. I married you, didn't I?'

'Only after telling me you couldn't afford to refuse,' he reminded her, 'and saying I'd bought out your objections.'

'Well, I had to keep up some sort of front,' she snapped, 'otherwise you'd have walked all over me, and, in any case, I *couldn't* afford! You'd seen to that, hadn't you?' She knew it was the wrong thing to say, it could start another fight, and she wished she could cut her tongue off because it was going on wagging and saying the most deplorable things. 'You'd cut the ground from under my feet, put me in a position where I *had* to do as you said. And you didn't believe me about the baby, you preferred to take the word ...'

'I've apologised for that.'

'No, you haven't, not properly!'

'Then I do now! Manon, my darling.' For a moment, Stephan bent over her, gazing into her eyes, but they were so full of tears he was just a misty blur in her vision, and then his mouth found hers and she trembled as the old familiar passion stirred into life and she felt the tremble of his body against hers. With a groan, he lifted his head and held her away from him.

'Stop grieving, my love,' he murmured huskily. 'We'll make another ...' and her stupid, unreasonable anger rose in a lump in her throat and burst, swamping her with heat.

'No, we won't!' she raged, beating impotently at his chest with clenched fists. 'I'm not having *my* child surrounded by bars, bolts and padlocks, so hemmed in he can't go for a walk without protection. I won't live like that. Fennie may tolerate it, but I won't have it for *my* child, and I won't let you take him away from me either. When I go he goes with me, so there!'

'But nobody's going anywhere.' Her spurts of temper went clean over the top of his head. 'We love each other, my dear.'

'Your kind of love? Ha!' She tried to turn her head away so that she wouldn't be seduced by the look in his eyes, but the duvet was bulky, it threatened to stifle her. 'I've heard you say things like that before,' she muttered savagely. 'Love? I've got another name for it! And you know what you can do with your blasted love, don't you? You can . . . Oh, words fail me.'

'Thank God for that! I was beginning to think you'd never run out of them,' Stephan coped with the bulky, downy mass easily, pushing it aside so that it slid away. 'Don't wriggle,' he told her sternly. 'You're quite safe, I've no designs on you at the moment.'

'Which makes a nice change,' she said sulkily as reaction set in. She could feel the anger oozing out of her, leaving her feeling beaten and weepy. She didn't want to cry and it was humiliating to feel tears gathering again in her eyes, but Stephan's arms were there and she found herself turning into them, grateful for their comfort. 'I'm sorry about this,' she gulped. 'It's the shock, I expect. I don't usually cry and I'm making your shirt wet.'

'Think nothing of it.' He sounded amused. 'I rather like it. I was getting tired of that "cool, hard lady" image you've been projecting lately. It's nice to have my Manon back.'

'That Manon was crazy.' She heaved a sigh of self-reproach and her voice was full of tears. 'I'm ashamed of me. Maybe I didn't break up a marriage after all, but I threw myself at the first man I fancied and I didn't stop to think. I had no self-control, I was as weak as water. If I'd been sensible . . .'

'. . . I wouldn't love you half as much,' murmured Stephan and his heart-stopping smile made her heart race. His hand slid to her breast and she felt the old, familiar ache as his fingers closed round it possessively. 'You still love me, I know! Darling, don't try to hide it any longer, you don't fool anybody but yourself.'

'You know too much,' Manon had no anger left. 'I ought to see a doctor,' she mumbled. 'I don't feel very well and I keep saying all the wrong things.'

'But you've already seen one,' Stephan raised his eyebrows. 'We called in at the surgery on the way home. Both you and Battle needed attention and the doctor gave you a dose of pain-killer. I expect that's what's making you a bit disconnected. Don't you remember?'

'Not much,' she admitted. 'Although now you mention it, I've a vague impression,' she groaned. 'What did he say?'

'Superficial injuries.' Was that a smile about his mouth? Damn him, he was laughing at her, and it made her mad.

'Superficial?' Her voice rose to a squeak. 'I feel half dead!'

'But you'll feel better soon,' Stephan comforted. 'The doctor also said you were lucky to get out of a car smash with so little damage. His candid opinion is that you're very resilient and as strong as a horse!'

Manon's mouth dropped open with shock. *'I was not in a car smash!'* she squealed indignantly as she pulled herself away from him and sat bolt upright on his knee. 'Your ex-wife pushed me over so I fell and hit my head, then she kicked me while I was helpless! *Twice!* Next thing, I suppose, you'll be telling me I was driving!'

'No, Battle was driving,' Stephan explained smoothly, and tempered the words with a smile that barely creased his cheek. 'And you were both very lucky, partly due to Battle's presence of mind when the steering jammed and you careered into the wood.'

'But that's not the truth.' Manon looked at him glassily. 'And you know it's not!'

'Mmm,' he nodded in agreement, 'but some things are better covered up.' He stroked the nightie away from her shoulder and bent to kiss it. 'That's the story I told Fennie, who, by the way, did the wisest thing when she found herself alone, and accepted a lift from the parents of another pupil. It's what I told Harry as well and I don't want it contradicted even though it's been unpleasant for you. You owe me something. None of this need have happened if you'd told me Linda had called here.'

'Battle and I decided it wasn't worth telling,' she mumbled obstinately. 'You were busy with other things.'

'Thank heaven you didn't include Violet in the conspiracy and she was still here when Harry and I came home to an empty house.' Stephan ignored her glittering eyes and her squeal of outrage. 'In future . . .'

'What future?' she demanded belligerently. 'According to you, there wasn't going to be one, not for me!'

'Of course there's going to be a future,' he said softly, making a promise of it, and Manon closed her eyes tightly on impossible dreams. He was at it

again, forecasting, managing, using her, arranging
her life to suit himself. She missed all the other
things he said except the last one. 'Had you another
reason for not telling me?'

'I didn't want to.' Her anger seeped away. 'Linda
brings out the worst in me and her calling here was
such a little thing,' she shrugged. 'I didn't want
anything spoiled . . . at times we seemed to be
getting on all right, but . . .'

'Only getting on all right?' His rare, real smile
curved his mouth tenderly. 'I thought we'd been
doing better than that.' He drew her closer, putting
a finger under her chin to raise her face to his. His
kiss was very gentle. 'Manon, my love, we *were*
doing better than just "all right", weren't we?'

'No!' She tried to close her mind to the seduction
in his voice.

'Yes, we were!' His finger traced a line from her
chin to her breast and he smiled as he felt her
tremble. 'Manon, we love each other. It's always
been that way, ever since Chichester.'

'No, we don't love each other,' she insisted
obstinately. 'We're just good together in bed, and
that's not enough. If you loved me you wouldn't
have schemed and plotted, reduced me to beggary
and then flung my poor baby in my face as a reason
for doing it. *No!*' She pushed vainly at his chest;
once he came too close she was lost and she knew it.

'Yes!' he contradicted quietly. 'We're husband
and wife, we're lovers; now it's time we started to be
friends as well.'

'Friends talk,' she sniffed. 'You don't, you give
orders. You make love, but you don't talk to me.'

'I can only ever think of one thing to say to you,' he murmured wickedly. "I love you". Would you find that too repetitious?'

They were so close together, she could feel the warm, slightly damp skin of his neck against her cheek and put up a tentative hand to touch it. The old magic was back, working its spell, and she flung caution to the winds. 'You could try,' she suggested boldly and with more than a touch of asperity, 'and if I ever get fed up with hearing it . . .?' she paused and shrugged. 'Actions are supposed to speak louder than words, or so I've been told, and they'd make a nice break in what could become a very boring conversation!'

'Will you be quiet!' But Stephan's hands were gentle as he shook her and she felt no pain. 'You're the most infuriating woman I've ever known,' he growled as he kissed her smiling mouth. 'I've just spent the best part of an hour telling you I love you. What more do you want, blood?'

'I want . . .' she began boldly, but her voice failed on a gulp of embarrassment and he laughed at her jeeringly.

'So I was right.' He relaxed and she felt the tension going out of him. 'You won't say what you want, but I will! You want me, you tell me that every time I touch you, and if you'd listen, you'd hear me telling you the same thing. Hell!' His voice rasped and Manon looked at him wonderingly; he wasn't calm any longer. 'You're in no condition for it, but you want me now!'

That touched her on the raw and she flared back at him with no attempt at denial. 'So! What's wrong with that? I'm a sex-maniac!'

'And I love you that way!' he groaned as he rose and carried her back to bed, and she nodded approvingly as he made a small detour en route to lock the door.

Manon stirred drowsily. She still ached, but it was bearable, and with a sigh of content, she snuggled closer to her sleeping husband. That was a nice word, and now it really meant something. If only . . . 'Linda,' she murmured, almost to herself, and watched his eyes flip open at once. 'What are we going to do about Linda?'

'Nothing, at least, *you* are going to do nothing.' Stephan was wide awake on the instant. 'I am! Tomorrow! I don't like playing dirty . . .'

'Oh, come on, do!' she muttered. 'You're a past master at it! What are you going to do tomorrow?'

'See Linda and explain.'

'Not without me!' she interrupted fiercely, her mutter developing into a sound very like a snarl. 'I don't trust . . .'

'This time, you'll trust *me*!' Stephan cupped her face in his hands and kissed her mouth firmly. 'As I said,' he grinned down into her bemused eyes. 'I shall go to see Linda and lay it on the line. There's no way she can touch a penny of Fennie's capital. It's all tied up for the next ten years and at the lowest interest rate I could find. Money's what I'm best at,' he added with a twinkle in his eyes.

'Second best,' Manon said generously; she was prepared to give credit where credit was due. 'Will that stop her?'

'It might if I also threaten to drop a few hints in the right quarter if she plays any more silly games.'

'Now *that's* what you're really best at, as I have reason to know!' she murmured annoyingly. 'What threats? I'm beginning to feel very sorry for Linda.'

'Spare your pity.' Stephan released her and rolled over on to his back, put his hands behind his head and stared up at the ceiling. 'Linda likes the social scene, the best restaurants, the best people, winter cruises, house-parties and all that sort of thing. One word in the right ear and there'd be no more invitations.'

'B—but why haven't you done this before?'

'Because I can't be sure it would work, even now when there's only the lure of the interest,' he admitted gravely. 'And there's also Fennie, my darling.' She watched his mouth tighten and saw the pain in his eyes. 'Carrying it through to the bitter end would involve a lot of adverse publicity, and Linda is Fennie's mother,' he explained gently, 'so for Fennie's sake, I'd rather hush everything up. What I'm contemplating is the last resort and one I'd prefer not to use. You see, Fennie doesn't remember her mother, she was too young when she walked out on us, and you've just said you were beginning to feel sorry for Linda. I'll have to take the chance that Fennie won't feel the same. You,' he turned his head and looked at her lovingly, 'you, I can cope with, but how does one cope with a child's loyalties when they're misguided?'

There was a long silence between them until Manon snuggled her small hand into his. 'All right,' she sighed. 'It wouldn't be fair, I can see that, so if

Linda won't agree, bring on the trip-wires, the mantraps and the security blankets, I can live with them if I have to.'

'You'd do that for me?'

'Walk over hot coals!' she said tersely. 'Fennie's worth it.' She gazed at him fondly. 'You're quite an honourable man, aren't you?'

'Honourable and uxorious,' he agreed. 'That means I love my wife to excess!'

'In that case,' she was beginning to feel weak and sentimental and she became tart to conceal it, 'perhaps you'd like to rewrite the terms of *our* contract. "As long as it takes" is a bit vague.'

'My love!' Stephan's arms were around her and she blinked tears from her lashes at the tenderness in his voice. 'Oh, my love. They were rewritten on our wedding night. For "as long as it takes" read "Till death us do part"! A life sentence.'

'Oh lord!' Manon closed her eyes and lay very still as if any movement might shatter the magic. 'The man's treated me like dirt, and now he wants everything.'

'The man intends to *have* everything,' he murmured softly into her ear before he gently bit it. 'Can you stand it?'

Manon dropped the last of her defences, she didn't need them any more. 'Silly,' she snuggled closer to him. 'I can stand anything, I love you!'

Coming Next Month

Available in July wherever paperback books are sold, or through Harlequin Reader Service:

In the U.S.
901 Fuhrmann Blvd.
P.O. Box 1397
Buffalo, N.Y. 14240-1397

In Canada
P.O. Box 603
Fort Erie, Ontario
L2A 5X3

Take 4 books & a surprise gift FREE

SPECIAL LIMITED-TIME OFFER

Mail to   **Harlequin Reader Service**®

In the U.S.   In Canada
901 Fuhrmann Blvd.   P.O. Box 609
P.O. Box 1394   Fort Erie, Ontario
Buffalo, N.Y. 14240-1394   L2A 5X3

YES! Please send me 4 free Harlequin Romance® novels and my free surprise gift. Then send me 8 brand-new novels every month as they come off the presses. Bill me at the low price of $1.99 each*—an 11% saving off the retail price. There are no shipping, handling or other hidden costs. There is no minimum number of books I must purchase. I can always return a shipment and cancel at any time. Even if I never buy another book from Harlequin, the 4 free novels and the surprise gift are mine to keep forever.   118 BPR BP7F

*Plus 89¢ postage and handling per shipment in Canada.

Name _____ (PLEASE PRINT)

Address _____ Apt. No. _____

City _____ State/Prov. _____ Zip/Postal Code _____

This offer is limited to one order per household and not valid to present subscribers. Price is subject to change.   DOR-SUB-1D

Carole Mortimer

Merlyn's Magic

She came to him from out of the storm and was drawn into his yearning arms—the tempestuous night held a magic all its own.

You've enjoyed Carole Mortimer's Harlequin Presents stories, and her previous bestseller, *Gypsy*.

Now, don't miss her latest, most exciting bestseller, *Merlyn's Magic*!

IN JULY

MERMG

All men wanted her,
but only one man would have her.

Desert Storm
Nan Ryan

Her cruel father had intended
Angie to marry a sinister cattle baron twice her age.
No one expected that she would fall in love with his
handsome, pleasure-loving cowboy son.

Theirs was a love no desert storm would quench.

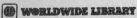